THE FIRST REVELATION

UNVEILING HISTORICAL SECRETS

SAHEEM HARIS

FanatiXx Publication
ISO 9001:2015 CERTIFIED

FanatiXx Publication
AM/56, Basanti Colony, Rourkela 769012, Odisha
ISO 9001:2015 CERTIFIED
Website: *www.fanatixxpublication.com*

© Copyright, 2023, Saheem Haris

All rights reserved. No part of this book may be reproduced, stored in a retrieval system, or transmitted, in any form by any means, electronic, mechanical, magnetic, optical, chemical, manual, photocopying, recording or otherwise, without prior written consent of the author.

"The First Revelation"
By: Saheem Haris
ISBN: 978-93-5605-191-1
1st Edition
Cover Design: Sagar Samal
Price: 180.00 INR
Printed and Typeset by: BooksClub.in

The opinions/ contents expressed in this book are solely of the author and do not represent the opinions/ stands/ thoughts of FanatiXx.

Disclaimer

This is a work of fiction. Names, characters, places, and incidents are either the product of author's imagination or have been used illustratively and any resemblance to any person, living or dead, events or locales is entirely coincidental.

Saheem Haris asserts all rights to be identified as the author of this work.

Preface

Christmas Eve. 2022.

Everyone was ready to welcome the festive season.

The streets were draped with lights in every color of the spectrum, which poured through tainted windows, causing some to doze off in the comfort of their bed. Others were just lying down with the light of their mobile screens flashing onto their faces. Not so far away, sitting in a cozy corner on the beach, was I, watching the waves crash against the shore, accompanied by the cry of seagulls behind them. The sound of the waves was like a melody to my ears, being played to rid my mind of all the stress and pain that life drowned me in, unrelentingly. I was at peace after a long, long time.

My thoughts soon wandered off.

I was born and raised a Muslim. Even as a child, I was pious, given my upbringing. I prayed regularly, which for Muslims is *salah*. Like every other kid in my hometown, I also received proper religious classes from a very young age and thus learned a lot about Islam. My parents later enrolled me in a Christian management school, it being one of the best in our locality. Therefore, I became familiar with the religion of Christianity. I never looked at it as a foreign concept altogether, but I just observed how they offered their prayers differently.

However, after joining medical school, I was intrigued by the different religions of the world. I was astonished by the wide variety of Gods and religious rituals that existed. This pushed me to dive into research on the same. The dark history of religious conflicts that were taking place even within my country disturbed me in every way. I was hounded by three profound questions.

    Is there a God?

> If there is, is it one god or many gods?
> Which is the true religion?

Time went by. I slowly started losing my faith. I stopped praying altogether. Worrying about a supernatural entity was the last thing on my mind. I realized that it was easier to live in the busy modern world as an Atheist. This went on till I reached my final year of medical school. Passing the final year exams is one of the greatest struggles in any medico's life. Countless hours spent in front of stacks of medical textbooks stressed me out to the point where I couldn't handle it anymore.

This led me to look for ways to cope with it. I started practicing yoga and meditation. I also slipped back into my old habit of performing the salah. As the days went by, I started performing the salah as a form of meditation. This did wonders. The few months preceding my exam were the most peaceful months of my life. While my friends were nerve-racked with the fear of the upcoming exams, I was in my room, fully confident and at peace.

I gave my exams and passed with ease.

I was finally a doctor.

Due to the hectic working hours during the one year of internship, I had no time to focus on my salah. I could feel myself seeping back into a void of pain and despair. Somehow, I managed to finish my internship and got the much-awaited license to practice as a doctor. This led to a big celebration in my house, with my parents by my side, eyes gleaming with pride, and other family members who showered me with words of praise.

I smiled through it all, for sake of my loved ones though being eaten up on the inside by a sinister question, 'What is wrong with me?'

I knew that salah and meditation had a lot to do with the bliss I enjoyed for a while. I started focusing on that again.

Right from my school days, I had taken a liking towards Physics. I spent most of my free time reading the latest scientific theories and these shook my understanding of reality to the core. I realized that no proper scientific theory ever disproves the existence of God. Moreover, I was able find many parallels between science and religion. This is when I decided to dedicate my time to further probe into theology. I restricted my entertainment hours and used them all for my new research. Fumbling through various religious scriptures and tons of research works, I was in awe of the unbiased teachings of every religion. I learned in-depth, to realize that to understand religion in toto, the field of history also has to be mastered. Therefore, I changed my focus to history, traveling through time, from humans who were fascinated by the discovery of fire to humans who ventured into the darkness of outer space. Months of hard work integrated with intense meditation and salah finally led me to a profound epiphany one day.

I snapped back from my train of thought. I was sitting in my favorite spot again. The waves looked more enticing than ever, gleaming under the shimmering light of the moon. I knew that I needed to let the world know about the historical facts that I came across and during my research the profound realizations that were churning inside my head. So, I decided to write this in the form of three books.

History lays the foundation of our understanding of the world that we live in. However, due to the rapid development of the discipline of archeology, many of the so-called historical truths that we were taught have been proved to be false and have changed through time. A proper study of archaeological findings can bring to light a lot of past mysteries that remain shrouded by falsely written historical records. Language also plays a huge role in preventing one from properly understanding a historical person or event. Names of people and places keep changing from one region to the other, due to the difference in language. A single person can be perceived as two completely different individuals. Therefore, by bringing together history, archeology and linguistics, many historical mysteries can be solved with ease. This book is the result of such an attempt.

The initial few stories of this book are infused with some elements of fantasy to provide an interesting start. However, all the chapters are based on data collected from the earliest theological manuscripts combined with historical data, backed up by archaeological findings in various parts of the world. The evolution of linguistics is also integrated into this mixture. There are a lot of names throughout this book, in the form of people, places, kingdoms and empires, which are all historically or theologically accurate. For this very reason, readers can get exhausted by a huge line of new characters and places being introduced continuously, but these play a pivotal role in history and thus couldn't be omitted.

One must finish each chapter by understanding the context, period and place in which the events take place to develop a continuity between the chapters. Various geographical maps will also be provided. Kindly refer to those for an improved understanding.

This book will take its readers on an odyssey through time, from the beginning of the eleventh millennium BCE to the present world, thereby unveiling some of the greatest mysteries in human history which still remain obscure. Through this journey, it aims to help them obtain a deeper understanding of the history of the world and the so-called mythical origins of the major world religions. You will come across various mind-boggling revelations in certain chapters, that can change your biased, preconceived notions of existing religions and which I hope, you will consider accepting with an open mind.

Happy reading.

Part One

Myth Or Real

Chapter One
The First Man

The year was 10,881 BCE. It was a day the Earth was closest to her lover and provider, the Sun, basking in his warmth. And hiding behind her was their beloved child, the Moon, shining with his full might, on a land enclosed by an ocean and guarded by two seas on either side. From the darkness encapsulated by two mighty fig trees, a loud cry arose, of a female hunter-gatherer who was on the verge of giving birth. The father of her child, who was supposed to be the sole protector of the family she always dreamed of, had been killed by a bear a few nights ago. Already bereaving the loss of her loved one, she was now writhing in pain from the life spouting between her legs, kindling the fire burning in her heart. With one last violent effort, she pushed a new human out of her worn-out body. A sudden burst of relief spread through her as she scooped the tiny creature into her warm blood-stained hands. It was a boy and she called him *Ah-Am*.

Growing up, Ah-Am enjoyed traversing various lands with his tribe. They would move often in search of food and water. The members of his tribe were astounded to learn he could stand with ease on two legs at the end of twelve lunar cycles and run around daintily at the end of twenty-four lunar cycles. Other kids of his age took a lot more cycles to achieve this. He was also exceptionally compassionate and empathetic for his age. However, on the completion of seventy-two lunar cycles, he lost his beloved mother in tribal warfare. This destroyed him. During the cycles that followed, Ah-Am was more reserved than he was before and kept to himself. He spent most nights sitting under the stars and looking up at the sky. His little mind often drifted off to the whereabouts of his mother and if she would ever come back.

The First Revelation

As he reached the end of two hundred fifty-two lunar cycles he grew into his strong, able-bodied self, highly skilled at gathering and tool-making. But the gnawing pain of loss he felt at a young age prevented him from ever taking any lives, even animal ones, so much so that he despised the concept of death. He kept asking himself, 'Why do people die?' So, he finally decided to leave his tribe to travel north following the *Da-Va* Star. The journey was perilous, but his mind was focused. After about seven lunar cycles, on a blazing hot day, he stopped in his tracks, mesmerized by a spectacular array of mountains. The mountains were coated with lush green grass and a wide variety of trees. It was the most beautiful sight he had come across in his life. He found a path between two mountains and proceeded through it. The path led him to an enormous lake surrounded by the mountains, holding crystal clear water that sparkled brilliantly under the golden rays of the Sun. It brought forth four mighty rivers under its roots which meandered in four different directions. He rushed towards the lake to quench his thirst. The water tasted like honey.

That was when his eyes met an enchanting island in the middle of the lake that looked like a widely spread-out garden. It was filled with flowers of colors that had never before fallen into his eyes. He jumped into the lake and swam towards the garden. There he saw another beautiful sight. It was a huge tree, emanating a powerful beam of light, angelic, almost. Its branches slithered skyward like snakes, covering almost all of the garden. He then walked towards the tree, astonished, taking in its dimensions and beauty. Eyes closed, cross-legged, resting each of his feet on the opposite thigh, he sat under the comfort of its shade, contemplating the same three questions over and over again.

'Where do we come from?'
'What is the meaning of this life?'
'What happens after death?'

Days passed around Ah-Am, but he kept at this ritual of his without food and drink.

The First Revelation

Then on one cool velvety night, he felt something inside him, swishing and swirling around. He could feel his eyes oscillating violently, one side to the other. Then, he felt himself being raised from the ground, and in a split second, his eyelids lifted with immense force. All he could see for the following few seconds was intense white light all around him. His vision soon returned to its normal state. He gazed around to find no change in his surroundings. That's when he realized that he no longer had possession of his body, lying on the ground. He was high up afloat, in the sky. Then he started being pulled forward involuntarily as if by some mystical force, accelerating at an immense speed. He could feel that he was going around a spherical object, which he then realized was the planet that he had been living on all these past lunar cycles. He questioned himself, "How did I understand this?"

Each second, he was making seven circles around the earth. On completing about forty-nine circles, he entered a human being and asked him the three questions he pondered upon. He exited the fellow's body and went on to the next person. After multiple such attempts, he could feel that with each person that he went into, he was planting the questions into their minds and simultaneously learning novel facts from them about his planet and various aspects of life on it, such as agriculture and herding, fishing, construction of buildings, pottery and trade, use of metals, mapping the stars to understand seasons and thus solar years, and even communication through words. He also tried to instill this knowledge into the people. He particularly spent more time in a group of people living on a set of mountains to the west. As time passed by, he started naming things. First, he named the Earth *Bu-mi*, the Moon *Šu-ma*, and the Sun *Šu-ya*. Then water was called *Ap-aš*, fire was called *An-al* and wind was called *Va-yu*. After a while, the stars were named *Ta-ra*, rivers as *Na-di* and trees *Ta-ru*. He even decided to name the groups of animals around. The cattle were called *De-nu*, sheep were called *De-ša* and goats were called *Še-ga*. But his favorite among the names that he invented was the name he later gave to God — *Aża*.

The First Revelation

This journey of his continued for about seven days and nights, and then he was back to the same place where he had started off. He saw his body still lying down there, in the same position as he had left it. Slowly he started to descend and went into his old body. He was a human again, with smoother skin and a more horizontally linear body, still twenty-one solar years old. He realized that his body also got bigger. But when he looked around, he was not able to see the garden anymore. The mountains were covered in ice. The lake had dried up and only a small portion of it remained. Even the majestic tree had withered and died. That is when he realized that seven thousand solar years had passed on Earth. The year was 3861 BCE. Suddenly another profound realization came to him, that everything in the universe, including him, had been created by a single invisible entity, and all this time he spent traversing the earth, imparting and gaining knowledge, he had been doing it as a spirit, which in reality was a part of this single entity. Only by raising spiritual energy could humans truly understand this entity and eventually be one with it. He decided to call this entity God. Then he asked himself, "How will I raise this spiritual energy?", and he said to himself, "Worship. Love. Good deeds." Using his brain, he needed to attain true knowledge through worship. Using his heart, he needed to be happy through love. Using his body, he needed to stay healthy through good deeds. And only when these three came together, could he truly understand God.

Feelings of happiness and peace were surging inside him. He knew for certain that it was not a dream. He traveled south for some time along one of the rivers. A sudden urge to keep travelling along this river valley overtook him. After having one last gaze at the majestic mountains that changed his life, he started his new journey. The sight of the tree kept entering into his mind. In his language, he decided to call the tree *Bo-Di*, the lake *Ka-Ši* and the garden *Ad-En*. With a newfound energy within him and high hopes for the future of humanity, he continued on his way.

Chapter Two
Good And Evil

After about fifteen days and nights of traveling alone without much rest, he decided to lie down by the riverside for a while. The river was flowing bright and free, guided by the calm breeze above her. He pushed himself to the ground and after aligning himself towards the clear sky above him, closed his eyes and tried to connect with God, as if enquiring about the path ahead. Entranced by the music of the flowing water and rustling leaves, he fell asleep. Suddenly he was startled by the feeling of some mystical force drawing towards him which was making his heart beat bizarrely. Opening his eyes, he sprang to his feet. He could see that something was walking towards him.

As it got closer, he could feel that his heart was pushing towards the chest with more force. But each beat was taking him into a newfangled trance of peace and serenity. The object appeared to be a woman and when she stopped, he saw her face. It was a woman with skin as white as milk and a smile as radiant as the moonlight. Even though he had never seen her before, he felt as if he had known her for a very long time. Both of them stood there for a while, enchanted by the sight that lay before them. In the next instant, they started running towards each other like the opposite poles of two strong magnets. All the trees and birds stood witness, and time itself came to a still, as these two magical beings danced in each other's embrace.

She tried talking to him by making sounds and moving her hands around, but he couldn't understand anything. Eyes glistening with hope, she then pointed towards herself and said "Ha-Va". And that he understood. He did the same and said "Ah-Am". Then she held his right

The First Revelation

hand and started walking towards the setting sun in the west. After this new journey of about three days, enjoying her beauty with each breath, he came across a few people that looked like her, fair and radiant. They looked very happy to see Ha-Va and welcomed Ah-Am with genial smiles on their faces. He understood that it was her tribe. Many people were living there along with lots of small children. They lived in houses made of stones and mud. They had small plots with a wide variety of crops and domesticated animals like cattle, sheep and goats.

Ah-Am easily integrated into the life of this newfound tribe. He learned their dialect, mostly just primitive sounds but which were different from his, and he helped them in their daily activities. He came to know that they were a very large group of people separated into six different cities a little far apart. The one he was living in was relatively new and smaller compared to the others. They had mastered the art of making advanced stone and copper tools. Ornaments and figures of animals were widely available. They even engaged in trade with local nomads and other settlements close by. But what surprised him the most was that occasionally he saw people standing in front of a big female statue, asking it for mundane things like better crop yields and more rain.

Ah-Am and Ha-Va lived a happy life together filled with love and respect. At first, they communicated with each other through sounds and hand movements. He then taught her the names of things that he had given. Thus, step by step, by combining these new names with their existing sign language, they developed a personal primitive language for communication. Through this Ah-Am understood that Hava's ancestors came from a group of mountains in the far west. Even though they spent most of their time together hugging and touching each other, Ah-Am was particularly adamant in his worship of God. He used to go to the river and immerse himself in it as a way of purification of his body. Then he would sit down with his legs crossed to worship Aża. Whenever he did all this, Hava would follow suit. Though he knew that she was doing it out of love, this truly astounded him. She also didn't pray in front of the statue. So, one day, Ah-Am decided to teach Ha-Va about God based on his understanding. However, to his surprise, Hava grasped the concept with ease just as the names of things. It was as if she was already familiar with the divine.

Years passed by, and their settlement developed along with their love. Ah-Am and Ha-Va who were Aham and Hava for each other now stood as the center of the settlement and its people. Aham tried to teach the people all the things that had learned including the names of things and the concept of God. They learned the names easily. But the idea of a formless God seemed too far ahead for them. Slowly, many of them started to believe that the world they see around them was created by a single entity. Still, they thought that the entity is the statue, and called her *De-Vi*. He didn't try to change it, as he knew that it was not about the name and only about submission to that entity. He knew deep down that they would eventually come to grasp the truth. He also taught them how to meditate and prostrate. With their help, Aham even built a small prayer house so that all the people in the tribe could pray together. He named it *Di-Ra*. His tribe had so much love and respect for Aham that they started seeing him as their leader and called him *Ma-Nu*, for *The Leader*.

The year was 3822. It was a cold winter night, and with the whole tribe waiting impatiently outside her house, Hava gave birth to a beautiful little boy. She named him *Ka-piż*. The whole tribe celebrated this birth. The following year, on a bright summer afternoon, the happiness of the tribe became twofold. Hava was blessed with another baby boy, and she named him *Ah-piż*. Both of them were young prodigies. They were brought up with lots of love and care, from both their parents as well as others. As they grew up, Ka-piż became an expert in agriculture and Ah-piż became an expert in herding. They helped their father in all his duties. Aham taught them about God and they easily grasped it. They in turn taught the young members of their tribe about God and showed them how to pray. They also made sure that nobody among

The First Revelation

their tribe worshipped objects or any other things other than the one Creator. Some started understanding the concept of an invisible God. But they pronounced Aża as *Aja*.

Aham was strict in his worship and ensured that his children took part in it too. At times he used to ask his children to give offerings to God outside of the Dira. Ah-piż always gave more offerings on his part and this greatly pleased his father. Also, the people in their tribe showed more affection and respect towards Ah-piż, as he was very compassionate and always helped others. This displeased Ka-piż, which later turned to envy and hatred. One day his father reprimanded him for his poor offerings and asked him to learn from his brother. Ka-piż's hatred grew to its peak. He went straight to Ah-piż with a huge stone and struck his little brother's head with all the force he could muster. Ah-piż fell to the ground, his body bleeding out. Once Ka-piż came to his senses, he cried out till the last thread of guilt left his body. When the news reached Aham, now furious and heartbroken, he bellowed in agony, ordering Ka-piż to leave their land and never set foot on it again. With the poison of the devil spreading with each step, Ka-piż set out to the east, to a land unknown.

Chapter Three
The Wandering Devil

The twenty-nine-year-old Ka-piż kept walking towards the setting sun as if he knew something was waiting for him there. Along the way, his mind was fueling itself with wrath for all the things he saw around him. After about three months of this journey, he was stopped by the present-day Yellow Sea which stretched out in front of him. From there, he traveled northward along the shore. Some more days passed till he came across a cluster of small houses along a riverbank. He walked towards it, and that is when he saw a group of nomads who looked a lot different from the people of his tribe. When he tried to approach them, they saw him as a threat and chased him away. But slowly, through multiple attempts and by helping them out in their work, he became a part of their tribe. Though they were using different sounds and words, he learned those with ease. However, in return, he never taught them anything about his ways of agriculture and living, even though it was a lot more advanced than theirs.

After a while, he found a female partner among them and through her he discovered the pleasure of making love. Soon she became pregnant. The lust-filled Ka-piż nevertheless kept on using her for his satisfaction.

At times, he used to contemplate the incident of killing his only brother. All these thoughts later culminated in a yearning to do it again. On the next new moon night, he was out with a fellow tribal man to collect some firewood. The craving to kill consumed him and the next thing he could remember was standing beside a lifeless human body lying in a pool of blood. He could feel himself smiling, with the same blood dripping down the flint knife in his left hand. Sadistic

The First Revelation

pleasure surged through him, thus paving the way for a killer in the making. Soon after, he began murdering a few of the tribe's adult male members one at a time. It turned into an obnoxious hobby until only very few were left. The tribe believed that the mysterious deaths and disappearances were due to attacks from wild animals. More females were available without a partner and Ka-piż saw this as an opportunity to quench his never-ending lust. One night, when he returned from a hunt, he heard the news that his firstborn child had made an entry into the world. When he realized that it was a female infant, he turned and walked away in disgust. He was least bothered to even glance at the tiny being that was formed from his blood. Instead, when the whole tribe was fast asleep, he sneaked in and took the neonate away to a nearby forest. The night grew darker as the stars faded in horror at the sight of a man burying his newborn child alive.

A few more months passed and another of his partners gave birth. This time it was a male child and he named him *Awan*. Despite becoming a father, he was still completely consumed with murderous rage. So, after five more years of living in that settlement and thereby exploiting it, he took Awan and left. Although this time, he traveled west along the valley of the Yellow River and continued his lifestyle with every group of nomads he encountered. He was glad that he had a child to use as an excuse to be easily accepted into the groups.

Fifteen years of this journey across present-day China and other small countries, through small settlements, thick forests and arid deserts, finally led him to another bigger settlement, a little far from the Arabian Sea. The land was blessed with two mighty rivers and this reminded him of his true home. It was the present-day region of Iraq. He continued his tyranny as with the other settlements. Within five years of diligent planning and effort, he conquered the entire settlement and became its leader. He continued with his killing spree, with only the survival of his progeny in mind. However, the native population also thrived with him. Later, his greed took charge and he started conquering nearby settlements. People began calling him as

The First Revelation

Ka-En. En was later used as a title to display his leadership. He thus built his first city and gave it his firstborn male child's name, Awan. By then Awan was twenty-five years old and he also adopted his father's way of life. He continued his father's legacy by naming his firstborn male child and his first conquered city, *Eridu*.

Years of ruling his people in vain took a toll on Kaen, thereby prompting him to lead a life of gluttony and commanding his servants to do trivial tasks for him. He spent the next fifteen years of his life whiling away time in this manner. One fine day he awoke from his slumber and decided to travel southwest. He then ordered Eridu to travel north, putting Awan in charge of his conquered land. He kept traveling until he came across another small settlement, where he lived for another ten years and then died on a new moon night at the age of one hundred twenty. His death was painful, but his soul beamed with pride, knowing very well that the ink of evil he had dropped throughout his journey would soon spread, and creep into every nook and cranny of the world.

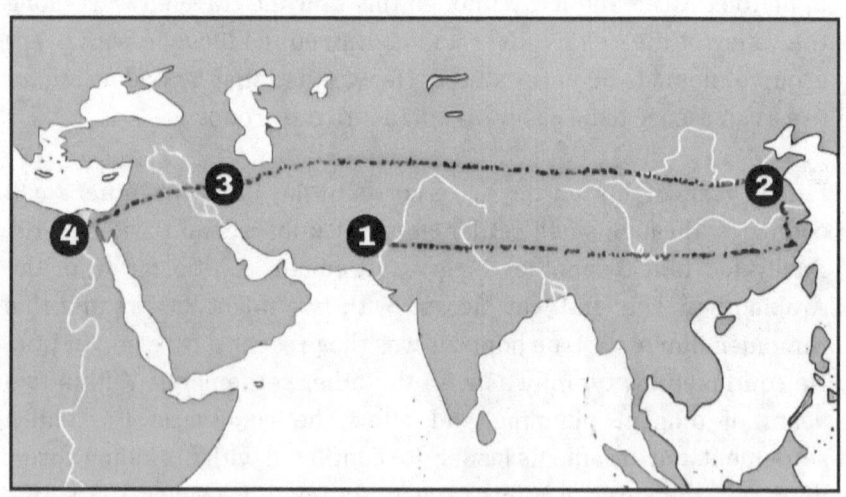

Path traced by Kapiż or Kaen during his long journey

Chapter Four
Planting The Seeds

The year was 3753 BCE. Both Aham and Hava aged slower compared to the rest of his tribe which accounted for Hava giving birth in her late fifties. But they had started showing signs of senility and thus came to accept the reality that they wouldn't have children anymore. Nevertheless, they prayed day and night to God, begging for another child. Miraculously the next year, a baby boy was born to them. It was a calm afternoon in spring. All the flowers and leaves danced to the tune of the wind, and the animals and birds chirped with joy. It was as if mother nature herself rejoiced at the birth of this precious child. The tribe members considered this child, a new bridge that would connect Aham to his future progenies and they suggested a name. He was called *Šetu*.

Shetu's birth brought about a drastic change in the whole tribe. The city started expanding itself and the people now called it *Nō-Ša-Ro*. The river that they held so dear to their hearts was called *Sin-Du*. They built houses of mud bricks rather than stones. Eventually, their city expanded to become the biggest in the province. People started migrating to Nausharo from the nearest city of Mehgarh. Soon, the latter was left completely abandoned. Caricatures were made on unbaked pieces of clay instead of rocks. When Shetu turned twenty-five, he found himself a partner. Her name was Shita. They started a family of their own with many children. After ten more years, both Aham and Hava died together in their house with Aham smiling in submission to the divine, lost in thought of Aden, the Kashi Lake and the Bodi tree, while Hava lay down with him, her head resting on the left side of his chest. The whole city mourned their passing for days.

The First Revelation

The death of his father left Shetu devastated. The day before he died, his father asked him to do three things. First, to believe in one God. Secondly, to worship this God regularly, show compassion to others and perform good deeds. The third and final, to spread this message to people all over the world. For the next decade, he taught all his children these three commands from Aham. He made sure that no portraits or statues of Aham were made as he feared that people could offer prayers to him out of reverence. Then Shetu destroyed the statue of Devi and asked the people to worship one God only. His mature children also aided him in this. Partners were chosen exclusively within the family for fear of losing their monotheistic culture.

And then one day, following an emotional farewell from his family and his tribe, Shetu left his hometown at the age of thirty-six and traveled west, accompanied by Shita and a few of their older children. After a tedious journey of four weeks, they reached a cluster of cities by a river valley. At the time Shetu was unaware that these cities were built by his long-lost older brother. He decided to start a new city to the southeast of this group of settlements adjacent to the sea and they named it Anshan. Shetu tried to spread the message of Monotheism to the neighbouring cities. Despite his best efforts, he was treated with hate and disgust, even getting physically harassed at times.

The area was still under the control of Awan, Kaen's son. Despite his advanced age, he remained the strongest man among his people. Awan despised Shetu and his preaching. In order to teach him a lesson, Awan decided to kidnap his beautiful wife, Shita. When Shetu was away from his home, engaging in his routine activities, Awan and his men abducted Shita and took her to his city. When Shetu came back home, he was completely devastated by the absence of his wife. With the help of a man from the nearby city of Kish, he came to know that she was kidnapped by Awan and his men. Steaming with fury, Shetu stormed into Awan's monumental house and demanded for Shita to be released. Awan agreed to release her if Shetu won a fight to the death against him. Knowing that there was no other way to get his beloved wife back, Shetu finally agreed. The fight commenced and it ended with Shetu standing on top of Awan's worn-out body like a valiant knight who came to save his princess. He then ordered for the release of his wife, holding a pointed spear against Awan's throat.

Over the years that followed, Shetu and his people built more settlements along the coastline. The whole civilization was comprised of Shetu's descendants, Kaen's descendants and the native majority called the Sumerians. This civilization became known as the Sumerian Civilization.

Shetu later returned to his birthplace and died there peacefully at the age of one-hundred-eleven, without knowing that true Monotheism would predominate in Sumerian culture through him only for a total of nine hundred twelve years. Though, six years before his death, another blessed child was born from his bloodline. The child was believed to be Shetu's doppelganger and thus named after his city, Anshan. Anshan resembled Shetu, not only in his appearance but also behavior. At the age of thirty-nine, just like Shetu, he too decided to travel far east to propagate the message of true Monotheism. With some of his brothers and their wives, he traversed day and night through difficult terrains. He had decided that he would end his journey only when he reached the vast ocean again. This took about a year, and they reached the coastal settlement of China that Kaen first sought. After years of hard work, they developed the settlement into a civilization and its people started warming up to Monotheism. It soon took over other forms of belief. They saw Anshan as a great teacher and called him *Shang*. The name they gave their God was *Di*. Anshan died peacefully among this group of people. Little did he know that they would revert to paganism and polytheism in the following millennia. Just like his ancestors, he also didn't allow for any sculptures or portraits of himself. Therefore, true Monotheism predominated in the area through him only for nine hundred five years.

The First Revelation

Then in the year of 3260 BCE, from the progeny of Shetu, Anukh was born. He traveled west with his brothers and reached the resting place of Kaen. Another civilization blossomed under his reign and he was called *Ankh*. He found many followers among these people, even after his death. Soon Monotheists became the dominant population. But in the year 2895 BCE, the progeny of Kaen came to power and slaughtered all of his Anukh's followers and descendants. They slowly changed his name and image into a symbol. Therefore, true Monotheism existed there through him only for a short span of three hundred sixty-five years.

Even though Kaen started the fires of evil all over the world, a few seeds of goodness too were planted in four different parts of it, which paved the way for the first four ancient river valley civilizations of the world. These seeds, however, were oblivious to how their stories would be told all over the world in different ways and through different names. Aham left a true legacy. He was the first enlightened individual, and thus the first Buddha. As he lived along the valley of river Sindhu (Indus), he was a Hindu. As his civilization was the root from where all of the future civilizations branched out, he deserves the titles of *Father of the World* and *Father of Ancient India*. But it never occurred to him that his people would become predominantly polytheistic and idol-worshiping, and would end up fighting with each other in the name of the very same God, to whom he gave the utmost respect.

The First Revelation

Earliest civilizations of human history

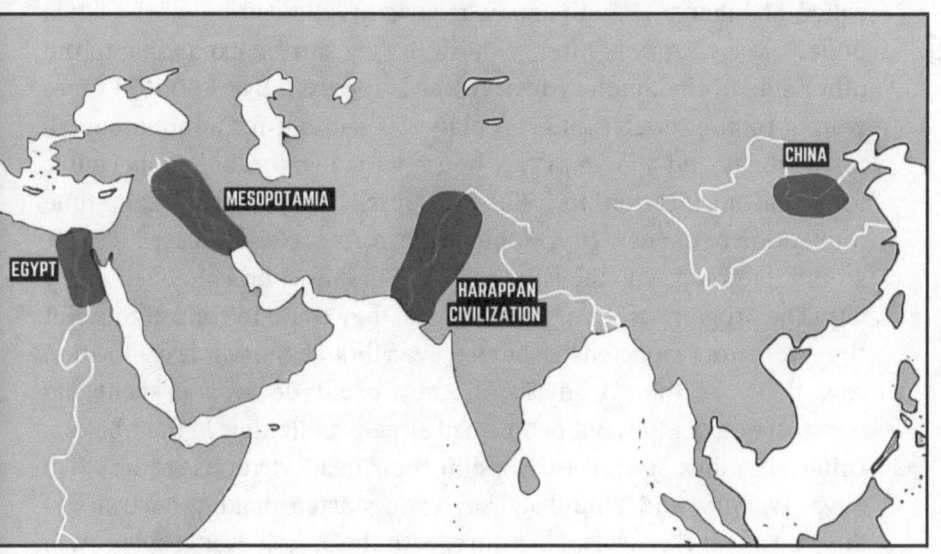

Chapter Five
The Great Deluge

After the death of Aham, his civilization thrived under the rule of his progeny. They now called their entire region of control as *Mel-Aham*, meaning *The High Place of Aham*. The inhabitants were thus called Meluhans. Monotheism was strictly followed by all the cities under the civilization. After 3500 BCE, they started expanding to the other side of the Sindhu River, towards the east. By 3000 BCE there were a total of twelve cities. A plan was laid out for a monumental, fortified city and a large prayer house with a water tank at its center for ritual purification. In 2900 BCE, bricks were laid for the stone foundation of the new city, Mohenjo-Daro. As society amassed wealth, so did its greed. Polytheism and idol worship soon colonized every city. The progeny of Shetu tried to do all they could to control this. But they were not respected like before, even though the whole civilization saw them as their leaders. All they could do was prevent the construction of idols. But people had already built idols in their hearts. Different tribes started to worship their dead virtuous leaders like Suva, Waddha and Yu-udha. They even started making portraits of Suva on small clay seals. Therefore, with the massive external growth of the civilization, the hearts of its people were getting corrupt.

Tensions were rising within the Sumerian Civilization too. The entire region of Sumeria was divided into two; the northwest was occupied and controlled by the progeny of Kaen, and the southeast was occupied by the progeny of Shetu. Sumerians who were the native dominant population lived among both these groups. Sumerians called the progeny of Shetu as *Anunnaki*, meaning *The Children of God*. The progeny of Kaen, who called themselves the Akkadians, kept on pestering the Sumerians and thus they started moving to the more peaceful southeastern settlements. This enraged the Akkadians. The cities of Awan and Anshan stood as a separate region further southeast, called Elam. Akkadians took hold of another city called Susa near Awan to strengthen their control over Elam. Awan was completely occupied by the Akkadians and Susa had Sumerians residing in it.

One night, when the whole city of Anshan was asleep, Akkadians from Awan sneaked in and torched many of the houses. Its inhabitants fled their houses in panic. They kept on with their attacks on Anshan and in the end, claimed it as their own in 2894 BCE. Thereby, the whole region of Elam came under the control of the Akkadians and they called it the state of Elam. The then-leader of Anshan was killed and others were tortured in various ways. They tossed a few people outside their own homes and occupied them. In the middle of all this mayhem, the next miraculous child was born among the Anunnaki in Anshan in 2826 BCE. People called him *Nōh*.

Nouh grew up bearing witness to the torture his people faced every day. At the age of thirty, he approached his people, urging them to react to this barbarian rule as a single force. He also travelled to nearby settlements of the Anunnaki. Thus, over the next few months, he gathered a large group of people, arranged some weapons, and surrounded the houses of the outsiders in Anshan. Scared for their lives, they fled for the nearby city of Susa. Then Nouh gathered the rest of the people in Anshan and surrounded the whole city of Susa. The Anunnaki were bigger in number and thus the Akkadians in Susa fled for Awan. Nouh then did the same with Awan and every single person fled, seeking refuge in the other cities of the northwest. Three cities were captured in a single day without any bloodshed. This was how the first true Monotheistic state got established in Elam.

The state of Elam with its cities Awan, Susa and Anshan

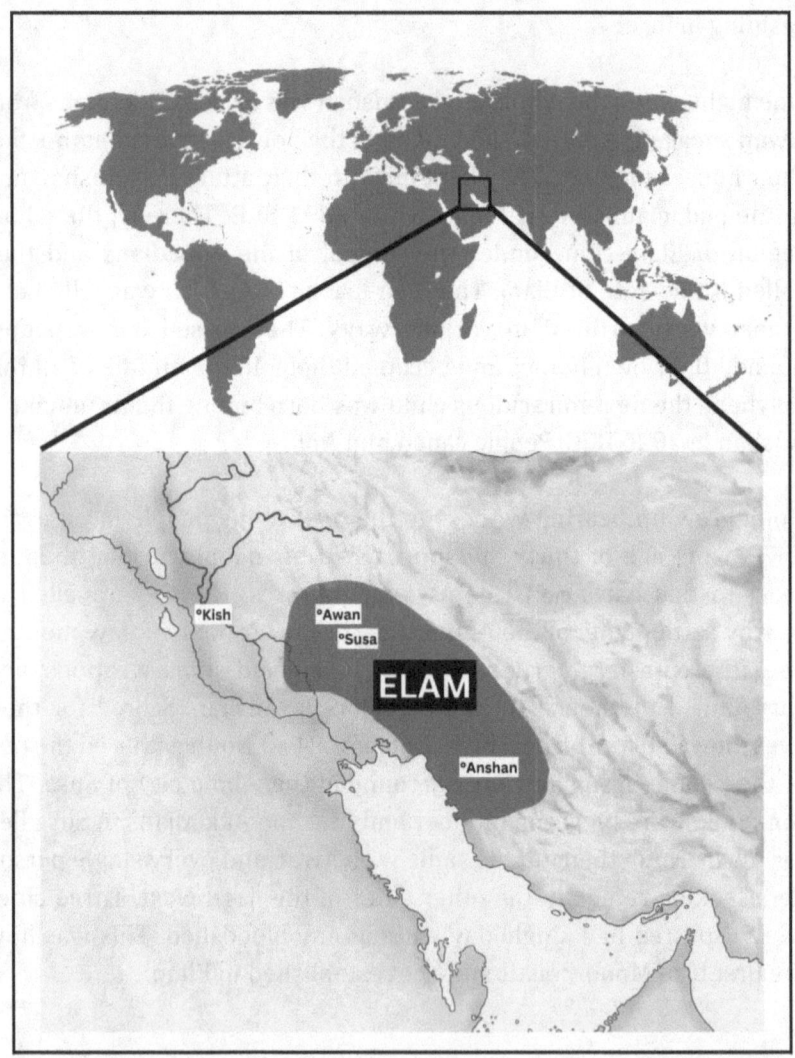

Over the next few decades, Nouh started teaching the Sumerians about true Monotheism. The people started calling God by the name *Anna*, as they couldn't pronounce Aża. He gained a lot of followers and thus Akkadians started losing control over many of the predominantly Sumerian cities that saw Nouh as their leader. The Akkadians lost their cities one after the other, including Eridu, which was their powerhouse. They were forced to move further northwest until they had to form a separate smaller state called Akkad. The Sumerians also got their own separate state which became a kingdom when they appointed Nouh as their king in 2784 BCE. They called him *Enmebaragesi* in the Sumerian language, meaning the *The Priest who became the King*. The Sumerians finally led a peaceful life and flourished under the rule of Nouh. They constructed a temple for their God Anna in their new capital city and named it *É-Anna*, for *The House of Anna*. It was during this time that the Sumerians started preparing wine from grapes, and writing also thrived in the kingdom.

Nouh found a partner for himself and they had six children — four sons and two daughters. One night, when Nouh was sleeping in his house, he had a dream. Someone approached him and informed him that his ancestral civilization would be devastated by a massive flood. This greatly disturbed him. After nine years of his reign, Nouh handed over his kingship to another fellow Anunnaki and left Sumer with his partner and children. Even though his heart was filled with despair, there was also a slight exhilaration of the unknown. He would be able to see the cities from his childhood stories that were built by his ancestors. But when he reached Melaham, that excitement went down the abyss. He saw an extremely polytheistic society, something his forefathers always stood against. Even some from his own family had drifted away from Monotheism. He gathered the still monotheistic members from the progeny of Shetu and decided to start preaching about the belief in one God. He taught them through certain hymns that he developed in their language. Years went by. Some people followed Nouh and his preaching, and they memorized the hymns. But others mocked him or avoided him completely. He then warned the people of the flood, but they just laughed at him. Even those who followed him didn't believe his warning of impending doom. The plant of ignorance had deep roots in the hearts of the Meluhans.

Finally, Nouh realized that there was nothing much he could do. So, he started with the construction of a huge ark on the outskirts of Melaham with the help of his family. Whoever saw him building the ark called him a lunatic. Still, he kept on trying to bring the people onto the path of true Monotheism. One day he had a tingling feeling of imminent danger, the flood. He made one last attempt to convince the people. Afterwards, he asked the true believers in his family and his people to board the ark. They did as they were told and took with them the domestic animals that belonged to them. They also had with them some provisions of food and water. But one of Nouh's sons had been misled into polytheism and thus he refused to follow Nouh. Even those followers who saw the flood story as a hoax did not agree to board the ark. Everyone that boarded stayed in it for the night. The very next morning they were awoken by the rain and the noise of people shouting in fear. A massive flood had struck Melaham. Many lives were taken by the flood, including that of Nouh's son. However, his followers and a few other Meluhans were able to flee by scurrying to the mountains. The flood water carried the ark with the people to the Arabian Sea. From there they took the sea route to Sumeria.

The whole kingdom of Sumeria welcomed Nouh and his family with music and love. Nouh was again appointed as the king and he peacefully ruled till his death in 2700 BCE. Through him, Monotheism predominated in Sumeria for nine hundred fifty years. His followers, along with the other Meluhans who escaped, returned to their flood-affected cities and started building them up again. Then they started spreading the teachings of Nouh within Melaham and also across the present-day Indian subcontinent, especially the south. Through his followers, the hymns of Nouh were verbally passed down through generations and made their way into the Vedic scriptures.

The First Revelation

Even though people later misinterpreted his hymns and created new gods out of them, his teachings of true Monotheism are still echoed in the Vedas. He was thus a prophet for two nations of people, Sumerians and ancient Indians. As the Vedas laid the foundation of Hinduism, he can be seen as the true *Father of Hinduism*. However, Hinduism can no longer be brought under the definition of a religion. It is a blanket term for a complex cultural phenomenon in India. It is a culmination of hundreds of religions with their separate gods, taken from different parts of the same scriptures, with its deepest roots lying in the Vedas.

Chapter Six
Razing A Civilization

Before his death, Nouh put his eldest son Shem in charge of Sumer. Sumer again flourished under their God Anna. The other two sons were obliged to settle in areas outside of Sumer to spread Monotheism. The second son Kham set out to the west of Sumer to start settlements along the coastline of the Mediterranean Sea. The youngest Yaphet set out to the eastern drylands across the mountains. This also led to the splitting of their ancestral language into other dialects.

What they didn't realize was that the Akkadians were making an army in their small state of Akkad. All the male members, including the children and elderly, were given weapons and armor to fight. And after a few centuries of preparation, in 2334 BCE, the Akkadians ambushed the city of Sumeria with full force. Hundreds of citizens were slaughtered, women and children included. Leaders of the Anunnaki were placed in captivity. Many were able to escape to Elam. The Akkadians thus formed the Akkadian Empire, commencing their rule over the Sumerians and thereby began diluting their culture. They turned Anna into a goddess and made her a partner of one of Akkadians' chief male gods.

Akkadian Empire at its greatest territorial extent in 2300 BCE

However, fate had its cards turned against the Akkadians in the form of another flood in 2226 BCE. The city of Elam was near the vast Zagros Mountains and so its people escaped easily. Anunnaki and Sumerians who mostly occupied the southern regions of Sumer also managed to flee. The Akkadians living in the north of Sumer, on the other hand, drowned brutally as it was a low-lying area. The few who survived had no option but to leave Sumer for Akkad. The Anunnaki and the Sumerians saw this as a great opportunity to take back their state and reformed their kingdom into an empire. During this period, a powerful leader arose among the Anunnaki.

He was a skilled swordsman and a great warrior. He formed a mighty army and put up a successful defense against the subsequent Akkadian attacks. His name was Nimrud. But the Sumerians called him *Ur-Nammu*. Later he became the ruler of Sumer in 2112 BCE till his death in 2094 BCE. During his short reign, he gathered so much love and respect from his people. Nimrud even built a great temple in the city of Ur, which later became known as the *Ziggurat of Ur*. He captured the city of Akkad and laid the foundations for a new state to its north called *Aššur* which later became Assyria. The Akkadians had no option but to flee further northwest of Akkad. Thus, under Nimrud, the Sumerian Kingdom grew into an Empire with the states of Assyria, Akkad, Sumer and Elam, which were all independently ruled by the progeny of Shetu through Nouh and Shem. He was also the first king to introduce a written legal code to raise the morality of people and for the proper governance of his empire.

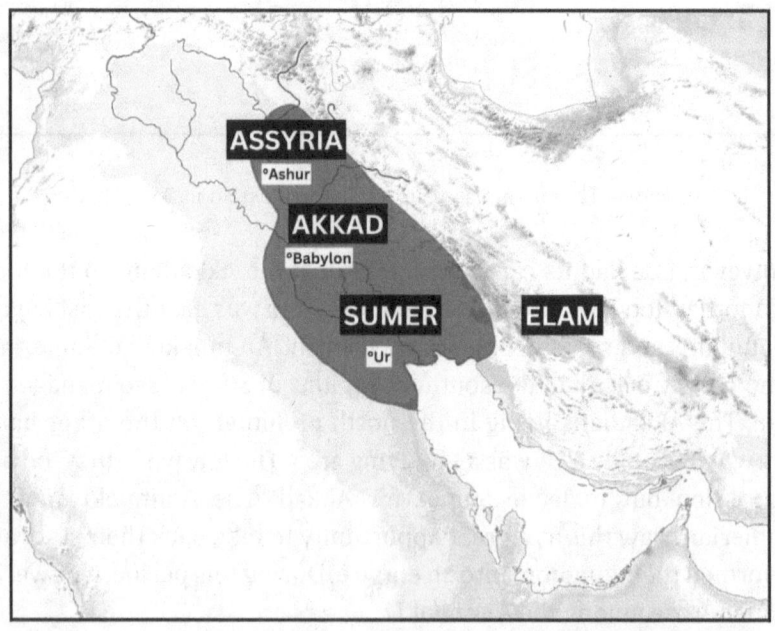

Neo-Sumerian Empire at its greatest territorial extent in 2100 BCE.

The Akkadians were a group of stubborn people who refused to accept defeat. They joined forces with a group of uncivilized nomads in the north and formed a cult known as the Hurrians. Similarly, in the west, they formed the cult of Amorites. These nomads were the trump cards for the Akkadians as they led multiple barbaric assaults on the Sumerian Empire over a few decades until it fell into the hands of the Akkadians again in 1894 BCE. The city of Babel was declared as the new capital and the entire region was renamed Babylon. Thus, the Akkadians became Babylonians and their new empire became the mighty Babylonian Empire.

Babylonian Empire in 1750 BCE

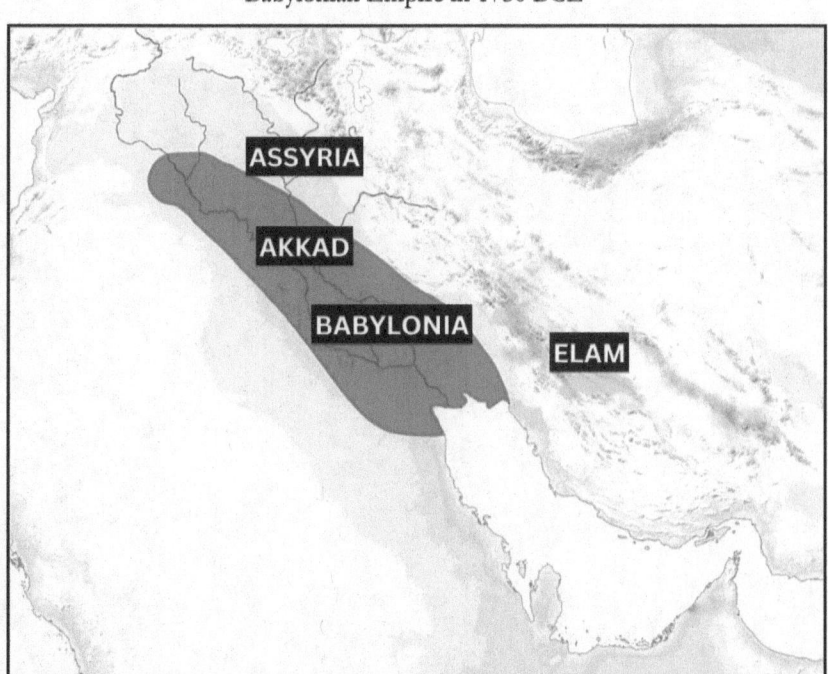

A wide variety of gods were introduced to the people and idol worship flourished in the empire. To prevent further revolts from Sumerians, all those who spoke the Sumerian language were executed one after the other. The state of Sumer was also dissolved and its regions came under Babylon. A great civilization that had endured the oppression of evil for more than two millennia thus perished along with its people.

However, the Babylonians were unaware of the Anunnaki that lived among them, who spoke both Sumerian and Akkadian apart from their native Semitic tongue.

Part Two

Ballad Of Wars

Chapter Seven
Father Of West

Monotheism almost became extinct in the Babylonian Empire. The Akkadians stuffed their temples with idols, and in the center of each one was a space for their most powerful gods, who came in a variety of sizes, qualities, and forms. They bowed and cried, begging and imploring their gods for help as if the idols could hear or understand these requests. Living under such conditions, even some of the Anunnaki digressed toward polytheism and idol worship. For those who were Monotheistic, life was hard. They were forced to live with their identities hidden in fear of persecution and death. The Akkadians grew so powerful that the Anunnaki living in the state of Elam couldn't dare to even raise a finger against them. That is when a new courageous individual arose from the Babylonian Empire.

Born in 1934 BCE in Babylon, the child lost his father at a very young age, due to the frequent attacks of the Akkadians. He was then taken under the care of his maternal uncle who lived in Assyria. A few years later, he lost his mother too. His uncle was a sculptor and an idol worshipper. Therefore, Monotheism was a foreign concept to him. During his early childhood, he observed that his uncle made many weird statues. One day, he inquired about them. His uncle responded that he made statues of gods. The child was astonished and spontaneously rejected the idea. He played with such statues, sitting on their backs as people do on the backs of donkeys and mules. He also used to hate his uncle for submitting to these idols. He never understood how an object could listen to someone's prayers.

When the Babylonians came to power, his uncle's business thrived. Frustrated by all the idols around him, he finally left his uncle's house at the age of forty and decided to live in the Zagros Mountains to the east of Assyria. He would spend many days and nights in the mountains trying to find out who the true God was among all. His mind was fixated on the movement of the stars. He considered what was beyond these stars and the moon, and was astonished that even these celestial bodies were worshipped by men. He followed the sunrise and the sunset every day. One night, he was sitting silently with his eyes closed, taking in the freshness of the cold breeze that flowed around him. Suddenly, he had an epiphany. He came to understand that there was only one God, an unobservable power that created everything, including the sun, moon, and stars.

At this point, he had made some acquaintances among the people who lived in those mountains by pitching tents. Their tribe was called Aram. They spoke primitive Aramaic which he found was very similar to his language. He realized that they were surprisingly civilized for a group of nomads. Little did he know that they were also the descendants of his ancestor Shem. He taught the Arameans the things he had learnt about God and he acquired followers among them. Thus, they called him *Ab-Aram*, Aramaic for *Father of Aram*. Abram eventually became an Aramean and the name Aża for God changed to *Aażah*.

Abram attempted to share his insight with the people of Babylon, only to be insulted and yelled at, like his ancestors. They even attempted to murder him by tossing him into a pit of fire. But Abram survived and he never gave up. He kept on trying to persuade the people into accepting true Monotheism. Eventually, he gathered a few followers from among the people of Babylon. The most faithful follower among them was Lut, his childhood friend and paternal cousin. He continued preaching till the news reached the ears of the king. The pagan king went into a fit of rage and banished him from the empire. Abram had no choice but to leave.

After leaving Babylon, he traveled west to reach Canaan. His faithful friend Lut accompanied him. Canaan was a nomadic settlement at the time. The Canaanites traced their root to Kham, Nouh's second son. From there they moved to Egypt. When Abram realized that the empire was highly polytheistic and pagan, he came back to Canaan and settled in the north. He then asked Lut to travel to the far east to preach to the people there. Lut followed his orders and started his journey. He traveled for months till he reached the boundaries of Melaham. Seeing the magnitude and degree of development of its cities, he stood in awe. He never knew that it was his ancestors that had laid the foundation of these highly evolved cities.

Lut pitched a tent outside one of the cities and decided to teach the Meluhans about true Monotheism. Lut faced the same experience as Nouh and Abram. He was even pelted with stones. He came to the realization that the people were wicked and cared for nothing but wealth. During one of his routine trips around the city, his eyes fell on a beautiful Meluhan woman. Later, he married her and they had two daughters. A few more years passed by. He was still not able to find a single follower from among the Meluhans. Even his wife was a polytheist and never listened to his preaching.

One day, Lut was performing his daily early morning prayers inside his tent. That is when he saw some source of light coming from outside. After finishing his prayer, he came out of his tent to have a look. He was perplexed by a brilliant cloud of light dropping from the sky towards Melaham. Trembling with fear, Lut rushed inside and woke up his wife and children and informed them that they had to leave immediately. His wife complained that he had gone mad and drifted back to sleep. With no time to lose, he took his daughters and fled Melaham. They kept running till they reached a small settlement. Lut fell to his knees, trying to catch his breath. Then he looked back, his eyes still engorged with fear. The light was no more. A few more days passed. Once he recovered from the trauma, he decided to return to Abram. After a journey of about two months, he was back in Canaan. The year was 1854 BCE.

The First Revelation

Abram kept on preaching true Monotheism among the Arameans. The Arameans dropped their nomadic lifestyle and grew to a very large population. With their help, Abram travelled to nearby settlements outside the Babylonian boundary and spread his teachings. He had many children. His firstborn son was Yishmael and his second son was Yitskhak. Before his death, Abram asked Yishmael to spread Monotheism in the Arabian Peninsula. Yitskhak was tasked with introducing Monotheism into the Babylonian Empire with the assistance and cooperation of the Arameans. Then Abram passed away peacefully in the presence of his family members and followers.

Three major monotheistic religions took their roots from his progeny. In Judaism, he is regarded as the founding father of the special relationship between the Jews and God. In Christianity, he is the spiritual progenitor of all believers, and in Islam, he is referred to as a friend of God and the father of prophets. In all of these religions, he acts as a vital link in the chain of prophets that begins with Adam. For this very reason, these three religions are together named after him, as *The Abrahamic Religions*.

Chapter Eight
Well Planned Conquest

Yishmael lived in the desert lands of Arabia and turned it into a prosperous nation through his descendants, as Abram foresaw. Like his father, Yitskhak lived as an Aramean in a small settlement to the north of Canaan. Following his father's wish to bring Monotheism into Babylonia, he kept sending his people there, under the cover of work and trade. But they were treated as outsiders and mercenaries.

Through Yitskhak, twin brothers Yakub and Eshau came to the world in 1762 BCE. Eshau later joined a nomadic group who called themselves the Hittites and became their leader. Under him, the Hittites settled and occupied the regions further north. Yakub was a great scholar of true Monotheism and thus became the leader of the Arameans. They called him *Isra-Aż*, Aramaic for *The Helper of God*.

The Arameans left no stone unturned to break into the Babylonian territory. Even though they were initially seen as a threat, they were soon hired as workers. This was a great breakthrough. Arameans slowly moved from their settlements and started settling in the southern regions of Babylonia. Under Yakub, they discreetly preached Monotheism and gained more followers. Then they gradually moved towards the north. At the same time, the Hittites under Eshau conducted routine raids in the northern part of Babylonia.

The Arameans allied with a very large group of nomads to the east of the Zagros Mountains, who had their eyes on the Babylonian Empire. This nomadic group poured onto the empire in very large numbers and sacked one city after the other. With their help and also with some help from the Anunnaki who still dominated Elam, the Arameans captured Babylonia in the year 1531 BCE. Based on a previously made agreement, the control of Babylon was given to this nomadic group.

The Akkadians, Amorites and Hurrians fled and settled further northwest. Some Amorites traveled to the land of Canaan and settled there. Thus, through the progeny of his son Yitskhak, Abram achieved the dream of bringing true Monotheism into the state of Babylon.

By then, another evil power had been rising in the west, the Egyptian Kingdom. They expanded towards the east and took Canaan under their control. The recently settled Amorites got appointed as the rulers. The Canaanites thus went through a phase of severe oppression. To the north of Canaan, some Arameans who were descendants of Yakub had already moved to Egypt to spread their teachings. It was in the year 1644 BCE. Unbeknownst to them, terror awaited them there.

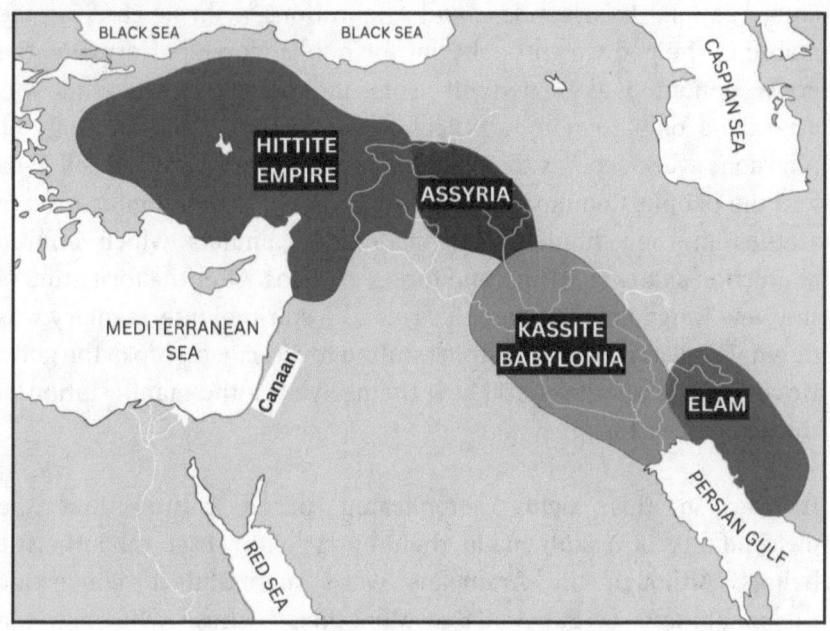

Kingdoms and empires in 1500 BCE

Chapter Nine
Splitting The Sea

The Egyptian pantheon was populated by a large number of gods who had supernatural powers. The structure of this pantheon changed according to the ruler as new personal deities got promoted in the hierarchy. Unlike other religions, priests made no attempt to create a cohesive framework that would unite the diverse and occasionally contradictory myths and stories. These myriad gods were worshipped in huge temples administered by priests acting on the king's behalf. At the center of the temple was the chief god of the royal family, placed in a shrine. Temples were not places of public worship or congregation. On select days and celebrations, a shrine carrying the statue of the god was brought out for public worship. Normally, the god's domain was sealed off from the outside world and was accessible only to temple officials and the royal family. Kings or pharaohs were seen as the spiritual intermediary between the gods and the people. Common citizens were limited to worshiping private statues in their homes. They also used amulets which offered protection against bad luck and forces of chaos. After the formation of the New Kingdom, the pharaoh's role as a spiritual intermediary was downplayed as religious customs shifted to direct worship of the gods. However, the pharaohs still saw themselves as the manifestation of the gods on earth.

It was in this highly complicated pagan culture that the descendants of Yakub made their entry with strict monotheistic beliefs. Although the Arameans were successful in converting the inhabitants of Babylonia to Monotheism, those who migrated to Egypt met with utter failure, to put it mildly. During this time, there was another group of slaves in Egypt. They were brought in from a cluster of nomadic desert settlements to the south of Canaan. These people were called Edomites and were larger in number compared to the descendants of Yakub. Both these diverse groups coalesced over decades to become a single community. The Edomites even accepted the concept of Monotheism. The chief God of Edomites was Yehowa. This got accepted as the name of the one true God of this newly formed community. The language of the descendants of Yakub also changed over time from Aramaic to primitive Hebrew.

The rulers of Egypt were absolute tyrants who oppressed the non-Egyptians. First, the non-Egyptians were kept in bondage and forced to work for hours for meagre wages. Then they were forced into slavery. Under this system, the people had no other alternative but to obey and worship the pharaoh. With the children being brought up in such an environment, their monotheistic culture slowly faded over generations.

Even being an enslaved minority, the descendants of Yakub and Edomites were increasing in population and, as a result, the Egyptian Pharaoh worried that they might ally themselves with Egypt's enemies. So, in 1296 BCE, the then pharaoh, Seti I ordered that all newborn children among the slave community should be killed. Scared for her three-month-old baby's life, one of the mothers placed her baby into a basket, went to the shore of the mighty Nile and laid the basket over its flowing water. The basket came to rest at the riverbank which skirted the royal palace. It was discovered by a palace servant who took it to the Pharaoh's daughter. She was a barren woman and thus decided to adopt the child, thinking that he was an Egyptian. He was named *Mōmes*, Egyptian for *Child of the water.*

Moumes grew up in the Egyptian royal family. But luckily for him, his mother was employed as a wet nurse to feed him. So, at the age of ten, through his older brother Aharon, he came to know that he was one of the descendants of Yakub. He visited his family in secret, whenever he got an opportunity.

The First Revelation

One day, when he was out in the main city, he saw one of his people being ruthlessly beaten by an Egyptian slavemaster. On seeing him, the person came to him and begged for help. Moumes became involved in the dispute. The slavemaster pushed him away and he fell to the ground. In a state of anger, Moumes dealt a crushing blow to the Egyptian, who died on the spot.

The news spread like wildfire. Someone from his people also began disseminating the information that he was not an Egyptian but rather a descendant of Yakub. Struck by regret and frightened of the consequences, he decided to leave Egypt at the age of thirteen. He changed his name to Moushe and travelled towards Midian, which was the nearest inhabited land. He travelled for eight nights, hiding during the day. The hot desert sand burned the soles of his feet. After crossing the main desert, he reached a watering hole outside Midian where two shepherdesses were watering their father's flocks. He helped them out. Upon hearing this news, their father invited Moushe to his home. The old man offered Moushe the job of taking care of his land and his sheep, which he gladly accepted. Thereby, he slowly became a part of this new tribe. After ten years, he married his master's oldest daughter.

Even though he appeared to be happy on the outside, the guilt of murder would keep him up at night. He would spend many days alone in the nearby mountains. His deep regret for the sin led him to prayer. He had learned about Monotheism through his brother Aharon. Days and nights passed by, with him in complete isolation in the middle of the vast desert, worshipping the one God and asking for forgiveness. His repentance eventually led him to a state of complete bliss and true understanding of God. Consequently, all of his sorrow got completely washed away. Then he made the sudden decision to return to Egypt. He wanted to save his people from slavery and guide the Egyptians into the path of true Monotheism.

Moushe returned to Egypt with his wife. Luckily for him, the Egyptians had long forgotten about the murder. He then met with his childhood friend and the new pharaoh, Ramesses II. To his relief, the pharaoh didn't recognize him and thus treated him courteously, thinking that he was a great scholar. He tried to teach the pharaoh about Monotheism. For a person who saw himself as God, this was viewed as an offence. He urged the pharaoh to at least release his people from slavery, but this was also turned down. When Moushe began to further challenge the pagan Egyptian belief system, he was expelled from the palace.

Moushe spent the next forty years of his life in Egypt teaching the Egyptians about Monotheism. As he could only speak the Egyptian language, he relied on Aharon to teach his people who had lost their faith. During this time Egypt fell prey to many natural calamities. But these calamities didn't affect the slave community. Though, the oppression that they faced started getting worse.

One early morning, Moushe gathered his people around. Aharon told them that they needed to leave Egypt and travel to Midian. Everyone initially dismissed this idea as ludicrous. Later, many were somehow convinced by Aharon. But a few decided not to undertake such a perilous journey. That same day, in the darkness of night, Moushe led his people out of the borders of Egypt and proceeded towards the deserts of Midian. By then the pharaoh became aware of their escape. He mobilized a huge army to pursue them.

Moushe and his people trudged through rugged terrains smeared by steep desert mountains. Then they came across a huge valley between this range of mountains. The choppy Red Sea was stroking the valley to the south. They crossed the valley and made camp at the other end. That is when they saw the Egyptian troops advancing towards them from the north through the valley. This led to widespread panic among the people of Yakub. Moushe and Aharon controlled them and ordered them to quickly climb the nearby tall mountain. Just when they reached the mountaintop, something miraculous happened. A gigantic wave from the Red Sea swept across the valley and swallowed the whole Egyptian force. Seeing this miracle with their own eyes, the people started signing verses of praise for their one true God.

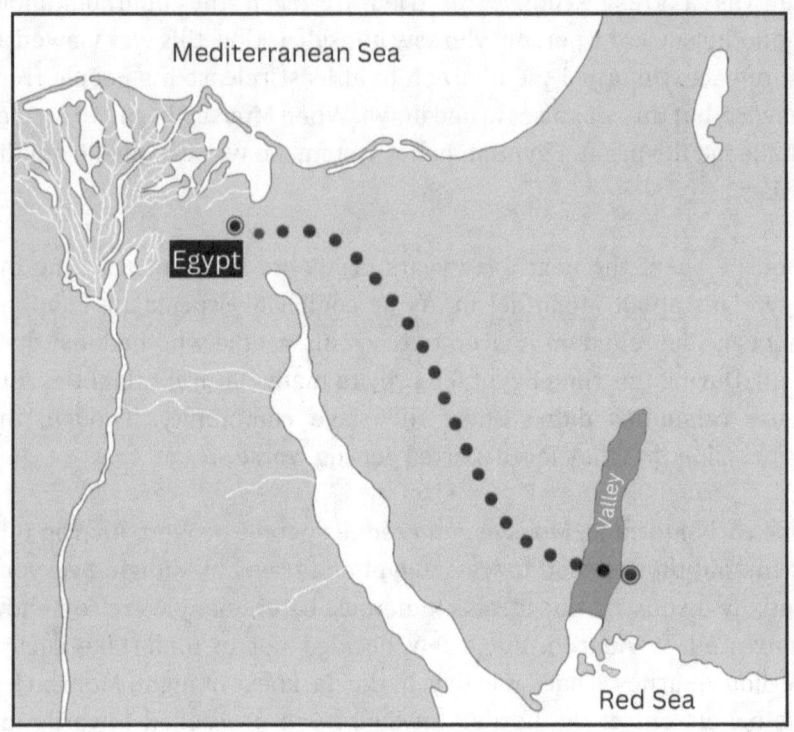

Exodus from Egypt to the crossing of the valley

From there, Moushe led them to the base of Mount Sinai and set up camp. Then he went up the mountain by himself. He stayed for two days, then came down on the third day and, via Aharon, gave them certain laws to be followed to improve their morale. Then he ascended the mountain again. This time, he took one from among them who could write. Moushe spent a total of forty days on the mountaintop without any food. He meditated and prayed to God through prostration. After forty days, he came down again, now with two stone tablets in his hands. These contained the Ten Commandments with a set of principles relating to ethics and worship.

Following this, Moushe turned away from the direction of Midian and led his people north, towards the land of the Edomites. On seeing their homeland, the Edomites dashed towards it with tears of joy. Although, to their dismay, only a few of their people had survived the periodic slaughter at the hands of the Egyptians. Moushe then led the descendants of Yakub towards their homeland. Upon arrival at its borders, they realized that their settlements were completely destroyed. The land had become a part of Canaan, governed by Amorites and subject to Egypt as a vassal state. They were denied entry into their homeland. So, they returned to the Edomites and started new settlements with them.

The year was 1176 BCE. Yakub's descendants had grown into a massive community with a vast population. They were divided into a total of twelve tribes. One day, Moushe assembled the tribes. After recalling their wanderings, he delivered the Ten Commandments by which they were supposed to live. He sang a hymn of praise, blessed the people, and delegated his leadership to the wisest among them. Then Moushe went up one of the mountains and looked over to the land of Canaan, his eyes filled with tears. He laid down on top of a flat rock and died, at the age of hundred and twenty.

The First Revelation

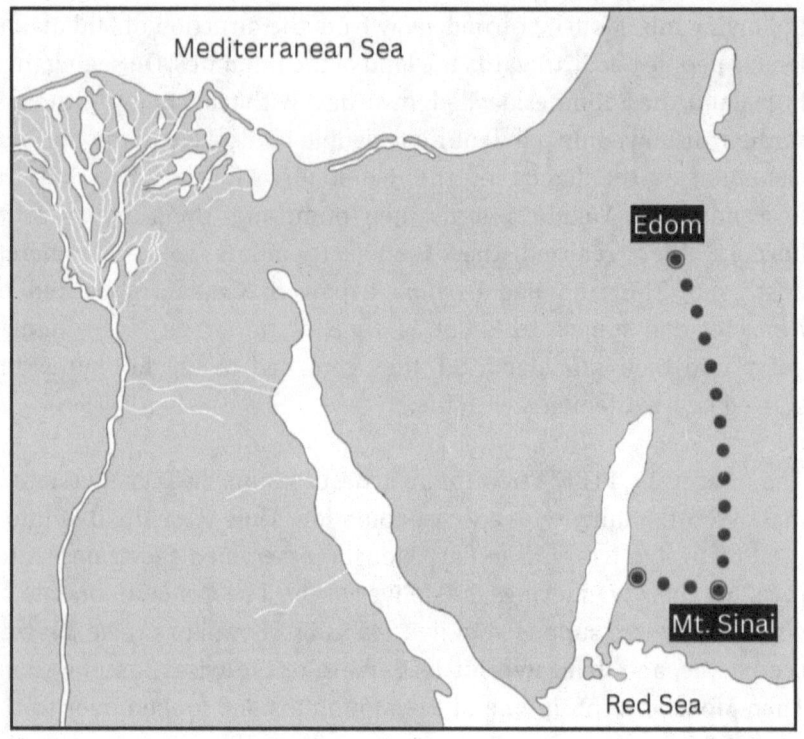

Exodus after crossing the valley to Mount Sinai, and from there to Edom

Following the incident near the Red Sea, the Egyptians addressed the escaped slave community as *The Sea People*. Just a year after Moushe's death, these Sea People attacked the southern regions of Egypt-occupied Canaan. They were joined by their fellow Edomites and also the group of Hittites who were already at constant war with the Egyptians. The Amorites eventually fled for their lives and Canaan was finally free. The descendants of Yakub finally reconquered their ancestral homeland in Canaan. They called the land Israel, as a token of respect for Yakub. This later developed to become the Kingdom of Israel. The kingdom flourished under some of the greatest rulers in history. However, the peace and unity that they initially enjoyed was short-lived. Soon there arose internal disputes among the twelve tribes and this led to a split into two separate kingdoms, the Kingdom of Israel in the north and the Kingdom of Judah in the south. There were also conflicts with the native Canaanite population. New gods started emerging on all sides. This later led to widespread polytheism and idolatry in the land.

Moushe's stories and teachings later were written down by the Israelites over centuries. They were then compiled together, giving birth to the sacred book of Judaism, the Torah. Over time his teachings lost their previous glory and got replaced by new ones introduced by certain rulers. But his valorous tale of saving his people from the clutches of evil rulers in Egypt still lives on, in the generations that followed. Both history and religious scriptures clearly point to him as *The Father of Judaism*.

Chapter Ten
Ping Pong Battle

The Akkadians along with the Amorites and the Hurrians, who fled to the northwest of Assyria, started expanding their power and territory. From the beginning of the fifteenth century to the end of the twelfth century BCE, they kept expanding to the west and the south, slowly destroying the Hittite Empire piece by piece and forming a new kingdom called the Kingdom of Mitanni. The Hittite Empire was later ruthlessly destroyed by them, and the Hittites were forced to settle as small kingdoms in the deserts to the east of the Kingdom of Israel. But the Anunnaki of Assyria kept pushing from the east. As a result, as they were expanding their territory to the southwest, they were losing their eastern lands.

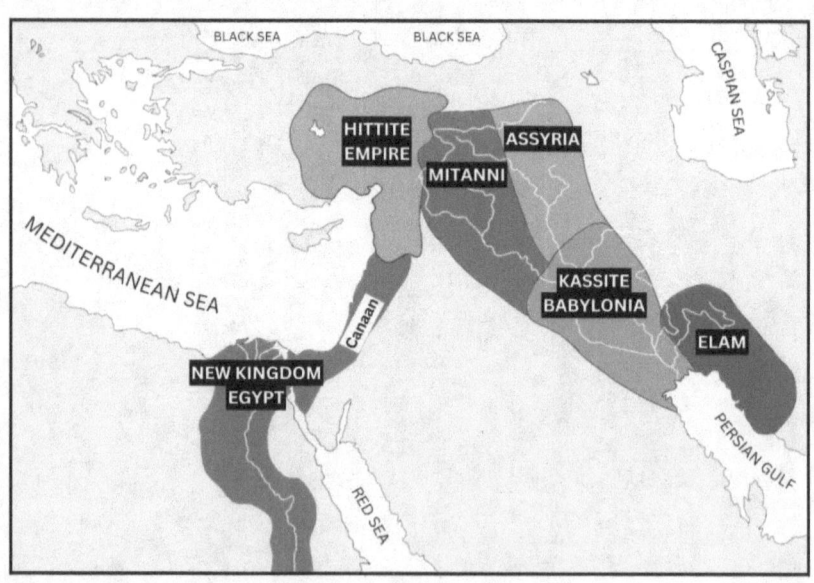

Kingdoms and empires in 1100 BCE

The First Revelation

The Anunnaki of Assyria slowly gained access to a lot of power. This greatly disturbed the Akkadians. As their kingdom was gradually destroyed from the east, the Akkadians fled further west. They joined forces with a large settlement built by a group of Armenian-speaking people called the Phrygians. The Phrygian Kingdom was thus established. In the process of fleeing from one settlement to the other, the Akkadians slowly started losing their language and culture.

Later, the Anunnaki expanded their kingdom drastically forming the Neo-Assyrian Empire in 911 BCE. As the hunger for power took hold of later kings, they went out on further hostile expansion campaigns, conquering the kingdoms of the Israelites and Hittites. They even brought the great Kingdom of Egypt under their grasp by 671 BCE.

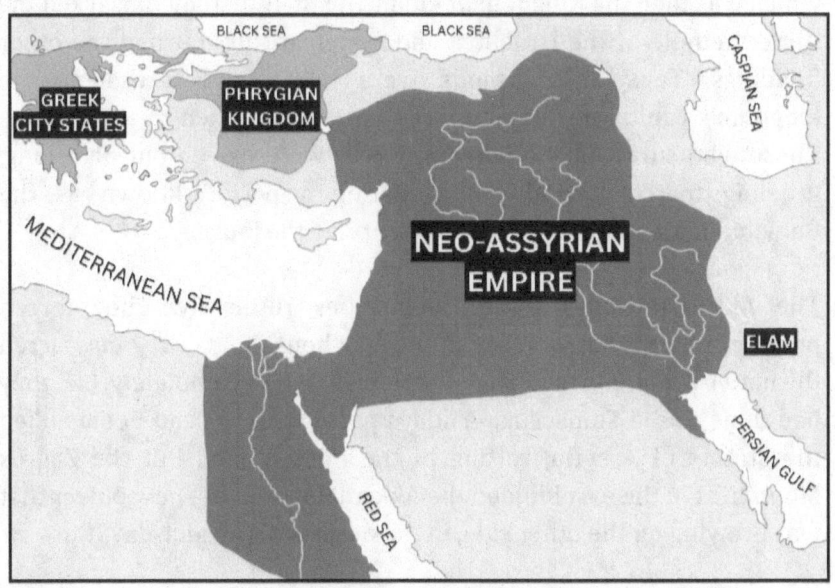

Neo-Assyrian Empire at its greatest extent in 671 BCE

When things were thought to be going well for the Assyrians, internal issues started to arise between them and the native Akkadians residing within the empire. A struggle ensued between their king and an Akkadian general. Finally, this turned into a huge civil war within the empire. With the help of the Phrygians from the west, the Akkadians took over their empire. Thus in 626 BCE, the Babylonian Empire was reformed by the Akkadians. Some of the Anunnaki managed to escape to Elam and further east. Though, for the others, it was hell.

During their reign, the Akkadians subjugated the cities dominated by the Anunnaki, which were mostly in Assyria. Under Nebuchadnezzar II, the Babylonian Empire reached the peak of its power. For the Akkadians, he was a true hero, but for others, he was the devil itself. After subsequent brutal assaults on the cities of Assyria, the Akkadians slowly started moving towards the western kingdom of the Israelites, which was then the Kingdom of Judah. In 586 BCE, they ransacked the sacred temple of the Israelites and systematically burned the other buildings. Tens of thousands were killed, and Jerusalem, the kingdom's capital for four-hundred years, was razed to the ground. Those who survived the horrors of war were driven out on a long, grueling march to Babylon, initiating a period known as the Babylonian Captivity. Many did not survive the journey.

The Akkadian kings treated minorities ruthlessly. They forced polytheism and idol worship into every household. They massacred the native Anunnaki to wipe out their civilization completely, like they had done to the Sumerians. As days passed, more dead bodies filled the streets of Assyria, rotting in the midday sun. But the Zagros Mountains in the east blinded the Akkadians from the new power that was brewing on the other side, in the deserts of present-day Iran.

The First Revelation

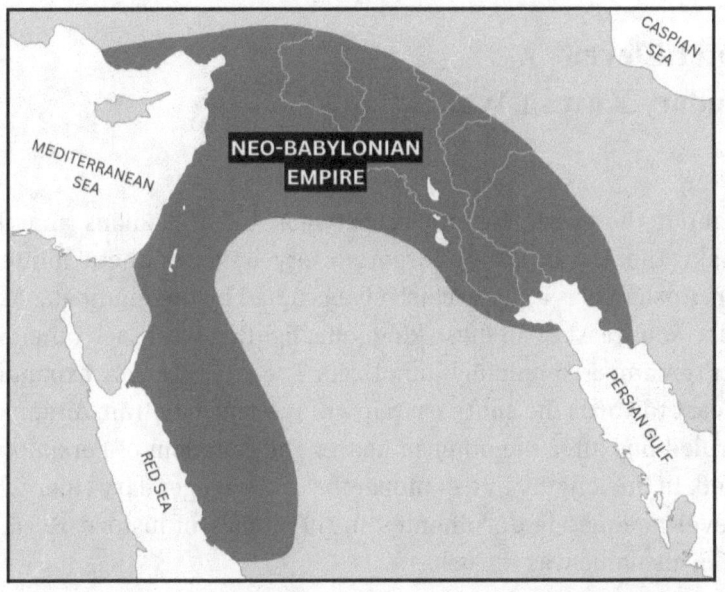

Neo-Babylonian Empire at its greatest extent in 550 BCE

Chapter Eleven
Legendary Kurush War

Throughout the tussle for power between the Akkadians and the Anunnaki, there was a long-forgotten city built by Shetu himself: Anshan. Anshan was a city exclusively occupied by the Anunnaki. As it lay to the southeast of all these kingdoms fighting with each other, its growth remained completely unnoticed. The city leisurely expanded to the east towards the southern parts of present-day Iran. Anunnaki kings ruled one after the other in peace. The Kingdom of Persia thus emerged. In the lengthy line of monarchs came a legendary ruler who was never adequately documented in the annals of history. Born in 621 BCE, his name was Kurush.

In the northern part of Iran, another kingdom popped up from a civilization that took shape around the mid-second millennium BCE. This civilization was also started by the Anunnaki through Yaphet, the third son of Nouh. The region which was initially called Madai later became the Median Empire under King Yuvashtra by the beginning of the 6th century BCE. The Median Empire always maintained cordial relations with the Kingdom of Persia.

Persia also had strong ties with fifteen other kingdoms to its east which occupied the present-day regions of Afghanistan, Pakistan and India. This connection persisted for about a millennium via trade and religion. The Vedic literature and its doctrines, which dominated the other kingdoms, had a significant impact on Persian culture. These kingdoms, together with Persia, functioned as a unified empire, but without an emperor. Because Persia was the most developed, its kings gained the most respect and hence functioned like the emperor. This harmonious connection was valued by the people for many generations as there were no wars or conflicts.

The only minor dispute that arose on occasion was regarding a vast tract of land that lay between the domains of two kingdoms. This territory was the one which was occupied by some of the finest ancient cities of Melaham. For many centuries, because of the inexplicable destruction of the cities, the people believed it was cursed. Forgetting about this curse, a huge conflict erupted between the two kingdoms for control of this territory, around the beginning of the sixth century BCE. Other kingdoms eventually joined in the conflict. Ultimately, an alliance was established by the ten western kingdoms, excluding Persia. They called themselves the Kauravas. The other five eastern kingdoms coalesced and became the Pandavas.

In the year 586 BCE, the Kauravas finally declared a full-fledged war on the Pandavas. With the destruction of their homelands knocking at their door, one of the kings of the Pandavas sent a messenger to Kurush, who now ruled the powerful Kingdom of Persia, requesting help. Kurush tried to establish a peace treaty between the two groups, but the Kauravas declined. After much thought Kurush thus decided to take the side of the Pandavas in the war. With the further expansion of his empire in mind, Yuvashtra also offered his help to Kurush.

In a rare month which witnessed three eclipses, the war commenced. It went on for eighteen days in the same cursed land of Melaham. Initially, both sides were showing no signs of retreat. With the Pandavas on one side and the elite army of Kurush on the other side, the Kauravas were finally forced to accept defeat. The majority of the Kauravan kings met their demise. The struggle over the cursed land was ultimately settled, and the Pandavas gained control of it. Yuvashtra seized the opportunity to accelerate his empire's expansion by annexing portions of the Kauravas' fragmented territories. This was followed by the coronation of his son as emperor of this new Median Empire, who would go on to be known in history by the name of Astyges.

The First Revelation

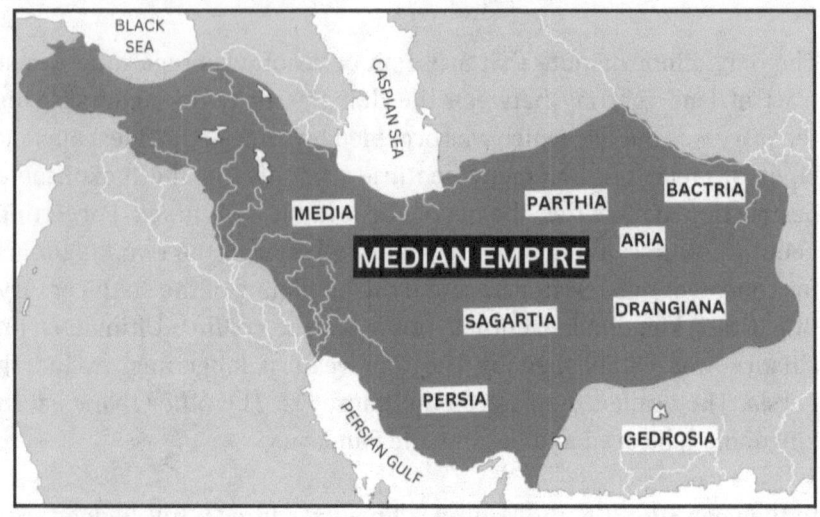

Median Empire after conquering the Kauravan kingdoms

This victorious battle left an indelible effect on Indian history. The five large eastern kingdoms were split into sixteen smaller ones as a memorial to it. These kingdoms were called the Mahajanapadas. Each kingdom acted as an oligarchic republic and the land of India thus flourished without any outside intervention for the few centuries that followed. During this period, India's first large cities arose after the demise of Melaham, thus leading to a phase called the second urbanization. The population of these cities increased significantly as a result of widespread migration from the west. Socioeconomic developments chiefly involved the use of iron tools in agriculture and the military, along with other religious and political developments. The political center also showed a shift from the west of the Indo-Gangetic plains to the eastern side.

Back in the west, Kurush and Astyges later strengthened their alliance through the marriage of their children. Kurush's elder son got married

The First Revelation

to one of Astyges's daughters. This union produced one of the greatest rulers in modern history, Cyrus the Great, whose true name was also Kurush, like his grandfather. After thirty-six years of his reign, Astyges had to abdicate the throne to his grandson Cyrus the Great, in 550 BCE.

In Iran and the rest of the world, Kurush's legacy remained overshadowed by that of his renowned grandson. His people eventually forgot the story of his triumphant war. However, in the land of India, the tale of the war was passed down through the generations. It became the main theme of *Mahabharata*, one of the two major Sanskrit epics of Hinduism. Kurush is still remembered and revered by millions of Indians as Lord Krishna, the divine being who helped the mighty Pandavas.

Chapter Twelve
Rise Of Persia

After the death of Kurush in 580 BCE, Astyges started adding more and more kingdoms which belonged to the shattered Kauravas. As his empire grew, his eyes started to drift towards Persia. In 559 BCE, he tried for a peaceful conquest of Persia which was then under the rule of his son-in-law. When this failed, he declared war on Persia. Astyges successfully killed his son-in-law and saw that the Kingdom of Persia was just within his reach. That is when his grandson showed his true strength. Cyrus successfully won all the battles against the Median Empire and finally overthrew Astyges to become the emperor in 550 BCE.

Once in power, Cyrus proved to be a great ruler to all the people in his kingdoms. But he couldn't sit around and watch the horrible condition of his fellow Anunnaki under the rule of the Babylonians. With some help from the Pandavas, he assembled a mammoth army and set out towards the east. Over the years, he conquered the cities to the north of the Babylonian Empire one by one. In the year 539 BCE, the nefarious Babylonian Empire had to bend its knee to Cyrus who thus formed the Achaemenid Empire.

The First Revelation

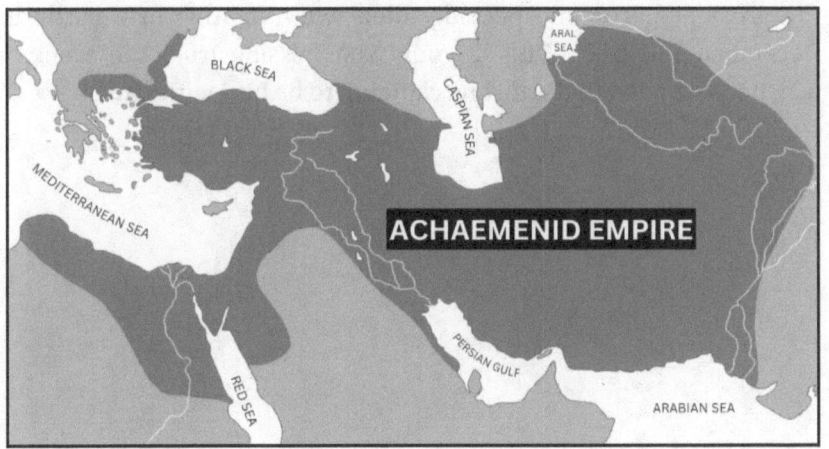

Achaemenid Empire at its greatest territorial extent in 500 BCE

Cyrus was known for respecting the customs and religions of the lands he conquered. Upon marching triumphantly into the city of Babylon, he made an unprecedented gesture that changed the fate of its people. Cyrus declared jubilantly that all captives who lived as minorities within the confines of Babylon were permitted to return to their homelands. For most individuals who had lived under harsh tyranny for decades, this felt like a dream. Cyrus became a true hero for these people. He also freed the people of Judah from their exile and authorized the reconstruction of much of Jerusalem, including their sacred temple.

The reign of Cyrus lasted about thirty years. A system of central administration was developed, which worked very effectively and profitably for both rulers and subjects within his empire. Under his rule, the empire embraced all of the previously civilized states of the ancient Near East, expanded vastly and eventually conquered most of Western Asia and much of Central Asia. Spanning from the Mediterranean Sea in the west to the Indus River in the east, the empire created by Cyrus was the largest the world had yet seen. Thus,

The First Revelation

his name got etched into the walls of history as Cyrus the Great. But the great emperor unexpectedly died while fighting in a battle in December 530 BCE. With his only son missing from the scene, a usurper ascended to the throne claiming to be his legitimate heir.

Chapter Thirteen
Road To Nirvana

In 553 BCE, during one of the battles against the Median Empire, Cyrus got into a confrontation with Spitamas, one of his personal friends and a well-known member of the empire. As the duel became heated, the only alternative left with Cyrus was to murder his beloved friend. Guilt-ridden, Cyrus made the decision to wed Spitamas' widow and adopt Damadutta, their eight-year-old child. Damadutta thus grew up in the Persian palace alongside Cyrus's other three children. Cyrus's only son Artashedda was the same age as Damadutta and thus they became the closest companions.

As the newly appointed crown prince, Artashedda resided contentedly within the ornate walls of his enormous palace. He had all that he could possibly need and maybe more. However, as he reached the age of twenty-one, the world outside his palace's gates began vying for his attention. He was curious about the lives of the people who lived within his empire. One day, his curiosity got the better of him and he ventured outside the palace walls. That was when he was confronted with the harsh realities of life, which had always remained hidden from him. He caught sight of people suffering from old age and numerous ailments. He also witnessed a dead body decaying on a street corner. Distressed and terrified, he rushed back to the safety of his palace. Still, the images kept haunting him for the years that followed.

While Cyrus was conquering one nation after another, he was oblivious of the plot brewing in the royal palace, to usurp his throne. When he overheard a plot to assassinate his only son Artashedda, he dispatched one of his trusted ministers to Persia, to keep the crown prince away from the palace for a while. There was nothing Artashedda could do but obey his father's orders and depart from the palace. What devastated him the most was the realization that he had to abandon his beloved wife and newborn son out of fear for their safety. Nonetheless, Artashedda viewed this as a chance to learn more about the anguish and suffering that permeated the daily lives of his people. In the dead of night, he left his home. As he slipped out silently into the darkness, he realized that he was being followed. It was Damadutta. Artashedda tried convincing his friend to go back. But Damadutta was adamant in accompanying him.

The two companions, both twenty-nine at the time, traveled east over the vast plains of the huge empire, eventually crossing the boundaries undetected. They continued their trek a bit farther and arrived in the stunning alpine terrains of Gandhara. The journey itself presented Artashedda with an entirely distinct spiritual experience. Over the next few years, he traveled through the forests of Gandhara with Damadutta, where he met two eminent masters of Vedic scriptures and meditation. He gained a lot of spiritual knowledge from them. He also became acquainted with a wide variety of meditative practices. Still, he was not completely satisfied. He rejected the Vedic teachings regarding rituals, caste system and religious sacrifices. He passionately thought that there must be a more robust way to explain the role of humans in the world.

Artashedda then shifted his focus to practicing ascetic techniques including minimal food intake, different forms of breath control and forceful mind control. He felt that by engaging in these activities, he would be able to find the answers to his questions. This led him to become so emaciated that his bones became visible through the skin. He kept on traveling from one place to another in between the long sessions of such self-mortification practices. Over the course of this quest for truth, he gained a few followers apart from Damadutta.

At one point, a previous memory came to his mind. He was a child, sitting under a tree, while his father was working on his combat skills. He then made the sudden decision to venture into the sizable mountain ranges close to Gandhara. There he found a beautiful land encircled by these mountains. A magnificent tree stood right at the center of the land. He went towards it and stood in awe, getting lost in its beauty. He sat under the tree and went into a meditative state, blocking out all the physical and mental distractions of the external world. After days of intense meditation, he finally understood God at the age of thirty-five. However, he was more concerned with the suffering and pain that people experienced in their lives. Through further meditation, he discovered the cause of this suffering, and also a way out of it. He decided to call it nirvana, a way of true liberation, by connecting with that one true creator entity through self-reflection.

He realized that the identification of an independent-self turned human beings into egotistical and self-absorbed creatures. It created an insatiable craving that enslaved humans to transient worldly concerns and kept them trapped in the material realm. If humans could extinguish this deep-seated delusion of the self, they would see things as they are. This was the way to liberation and the end of suffering. He also realized that only by mastering this idea can one truly understand God. So, he decided to focus on the practical solutions to overcome the attachment to this material realm rather than on the more complex spiritual realm of God.

With the help of Damadutta, Artashedda began disseminating this newfound wisdom across Gandhara. In a short duration of time, he gathered a sizable following, and his popularity spread to the neighboring kingdoms. In their native Pali language, the Gandharan populace began referring to him as *Gotama*, which meant *The bright light*. The followers called themselves the Sakas. It was during this period that Artashedda came to know of his father's death. The year was 530 BCE. He longed to see him one last time before the body was buried. However, through his supporters, he discovered that all of his father's loyal ministers and commanders had been assassinated and that a Kauravan monarch from inside their empire had risen to the throne by claiming to be one of his sons. Artashedda no longer had any desire in him to be an emperor. Therefore, he strengthened his mind and focused on his teachings.

Chapter Fourteen
Begetting Two Religions

Artashedda's teachings spread like wildfire throughout the Achaemenid Empire. The regime particularly gained greater power in the eastern parts, due to the presence of Gandhara. This was the time when a young Kauravan ruler, Darius, had his sights set on the throne. In 522 BCE, he discreetly assassinated the then-emperor and planned to take the throne. Damadutta had always held Artashedda to be the legitimate successor to the empire. Using the help of some of their followers, he took control of the empire in the name of Artashedda for seven months. Nevertheless, Artashedda, who had always been reluctant to reveal his actual identity, refuted the assertion and persuaded Damadutta to step down. Damadutta was quite frustrated by this. Darius was thus crowned emperor.

Darius was well aware that Artashedda posed a significant threat to his throne. With the help of some spies, he discovered that Artashedda was actually the son of Cyrus and Damadutta was the son of Spitamas. An idea came into his mind. He conquered Gandhara and its surrounding regions. Darius, accompanied by his father, then approached Damadutta and told him the truth regarding his true father's demise. Damadutta, who was already vexed, started boiling with rage. He split from Artashedda's group and formed a competing sect with the support of Darius. This new sect was centered around the Kingdom of Bactria, which was a stronghold of Artashedda's followers. They used Artashedda's teachings and prepared manuscripts in the native Avestan language of Bactria, by making a few changes and adding some Avestan names.

Damadutta thus became one of the greatest mythological figures in

The First Revelation

history, by the name Zoroaster, the prophet who spread the religion of Zoroastrianism. Since it began as a strictly monotheistic religion, it was largely embraced by the populace of the Achaemenid Empire. Its teachings easily traversed throughout the empire with the help of Darius. With the exception of the eastern regions, where Artashedda's teachings continued to be dominant, Zoroastrianism quickly became the dominant belief system within the empire. Darius then killed Damadutta, for he posed a threat as well.

During Darius' reign, his son also began to gain prominence. The followers of Artashedda were becoming more powerful by the minute. To eliminate the growing threat, a military operation led by Darius' son was organized against him and his followers. Across all of Gandhara, there was a bounty placed on his head. Artashedda managed to escape with some of his followers at the age of sixty-six. A large portion of his supporters was brutally murdered, and his writings were burned. Even after ascending to the throne as emperor, Darius's son made every effort to keep Artashedda's teachings out of his empire.

Artashedda journeyed southeast along the valley of the great Himalayas, eventually finding refuge in one of the kingdoms of the majestic land of India. Even as old age began to take its toll on him, he continued to travel and teach people. The prevalent caste structure in the community deeply bothered him. He even spoke against the dominance of the priestly caste of Brahmins over other sections of society. He endured criticism for this precise reason, and thus he was only able to gather a small number of supporters in India. Later, in the year 481 BCE, Artashedda left the world of suffering behind him and returned to the spiritual realm by uniting with the entire cosmos, achieving ultimate nirvana.

The avarice of certain historically corrupt monarchs led to the destruction of some of Artashedda's authentic written teachings. Even so, many survived as they were maintained orally by his surviving adherents, mostly in the eastern parts of the Achaemenid Empire itself. The kingdom expanded over centuries, and Buddhism was born. Influenced by Arthashedda's doctrines, King Ashoka attempted to promulgate Buddhism within his vast empire by integrating it with the dominant Vedic teachings. In this process, a significant chunk of its message was grossly mistranslated.

Unlike other languages, Persian was written from right to left. As a result, in other languages, Artashedda's name was first written as Sheddarta and later it became Siddhartha. However, he became famous all over the world by the name of Buddha, the awakened one. Zoroastrians still perceive Zoroaster to be their prophet. But they remain unaware of the fact that Buddha himself was their true prophet since the religion is almost completely based on his teachings. So, Buddha's earliest teachings also survived through Zoroastrianism. This was how a man from Persia, a descendant of Aham or the First Mahasammata, became the Father of two different religious communities.

Chapter Fifteen
Devil's Mighty Empire

Around the beginning of the eighth century BCE, the Akkadians and Phrygians saw resource-rich tribal lands on the west across the Aegon Sea. Thus, they migrated to these lands and kept on expanding their number with their base as the Kingdom of Phrygia. Native nomads and tribal people were slaughtered, and cities like Sparta, Athens and Macedonia sprouted with their blood as manure. Women alone were spared for the purpose of procreation. The Akkadians alone ventured further west and built a small isolated city named Rome. With the fall of the Neo-Babylonian Empire, Akkadians flooded the cities of that region. These cities thus steadily grew into city-states and later, kingdoms.

By the year 336 BCE the Kingdom of Macedonia subdued the others and became a superpower. The most powerful Macedonian King, Alexander the Great, came to power and overthrew the Achaemenid Empire during the following years. In the year 326 BCE, Alexander created one of the largest empires in history, stretching from Greece to northwestern India. He was undefeated in battle and became one of the most successful military commanders in history. In the years following his death in 323 BCE, a series of civil wars broke out across the Macedonian Empire, eventually leading to its disintegration. New empires arose under the Generals of Alexander and other kings. But they never would have foreseen the formidable force that was contained within the walls of the city of Rome.

As the city of Rome developed, it was ruled by kings. The kings possessed ultimate executive power and unchecked military authority. They even acted as mediators between the Roman gods and the people. But under these kings, Rome suffered through a bout of domestic crisis. Some of the people organized themselves and initiated a revolution against the existing monarchy. The Roman monarchy was thus overthrown and replaced by the Roman Republic in 509 BCE.

The Roman Republic was a form of government run through a public representation of the people. Roman society under the republic was primarily a mix of various cultures. Its political organization developed with a collective and annual magistrate, overseen by a senate. Under its administration, Rome's control rapidly expanded from the city's immediate surroundings to the entire Mediterranean region. Later on, it embarked on a long series of conquests, bringing down its rival empires one after the other.

The Roman Republic became severely destabilized by civil wars and political conflicts. The great generals started exploiting their power and fighting against each other for the land. In the middle of the first century BCE, Julius Caesar was appointed as the dictator. He was later stabbed to death by a group of rebellious senators. Civil wars and proscriptions continued, eventually culminating in the victory of Octavian, Caesar's adopted son. The following year, Octavian conquered the Kingdom of Egypt. Octavian's power became unassailable and the Roman Senate granted him overarching powers, making him the first Roman emperor in 27 BCE. A brief period of stable representative democracy thus collapsed and the system of monarchy returned to the west.

Roman Empire at its greatest territorial extent in 117 CE

Part Three

Painting The Present

Chapter Sixteen
Virgin Gives Birth

By the end of the first century BCE, the Roman Empire quickly spread across the Mediterranean, sweeping through North Africa and reaching as far as Spain in the west. To the east, it encompassed Egypt, Turkey, Greece and Palestine. In the Roman province of Palestine was Jerusalem, the holy land of the Jews. Along the coastline, a forty-mile-long aqueduct was constructed. It brought water to a newly built seaport which became a city. In honor of the Roman Emperor, the city was named Caesarea. In the thriving seaport, the power of Rome along with its culture and commerce commanded every aspect of daily life. Into this political climate, in the year 3 CE, in the fertile mountainous region of Galilee, a divine child was born miraculously of a virgin woman. His name was Yeshua.

Yeshua grew up in the village of Nazareth, about seven miles from his place of birth. The village was thoroughly Jewish. As years passed, his intelligence and compassion began to augment. When he was twelve years old, he accompanied his mother to Jerusalem. There he wandered into the temple and joined a crowd listening to the lecture of the Jewish Priests. The audience was all adults, but he was not afraid to sit with them. After listening intently, he asked questions and expressed his opinion. The learned clerics were disturbed by the boy's boldness and puzzled by the questions he asked, for they were unable to answer him. They tried to silence him, but he ignored their attempts and continued to express his views. Yeshua became so involved in this exchange that he forgot he was expected back home.

Yeshua remained faithful to his religious heritage throughout his childhood. Being from the lineage of Abram, his mother, Mary, was

The First Revelation

well-versed in the Torah and its teachings. She was Yeshua's first teacher. He was particularly influenced by one of his close relatives, John the Baptist. John belonged to an apocalyptic sect of Judaism that refused to immerse itself in public life. With few exceptions, they shunned temple worship and were content to live as ascetics performing manual labor in seclusion. Even though they were considered extremists, they preserved some of the true teachings of their religion. Yeshua was slowly attracted to their beliefs and teachings. He thus started spending more of his time with John, out in the deserts, learning in depth about his religion and God. Having no father of his own, he started seeing God as a fatherly figure.

Yeshua had this intense desire within him to learn about other cultures and beliefs. At the age of thirteen, he left his home before the sun peaked through the horizon, and joined a group of merchants who had embarked on a long journey eastward. With their help, he reached the region of present-day India. He travelled across India, learning about its diverse cultures and religious practices. The Vedic scriptures had a significant influence on him. His interests shifted more towards Ayurveda, the use of herbal therapy to treat ailments. He was astounded by how a combination of herbs could treat many diseases that were thought to be incurable. Even though he adored the Vedic texts, the culture that it gave birth to distressed him, which included the caste system and idolatry that was prominent among the people. He tried teaching the people about Monotheism. But the priests and religious fanatics mistreated and abused him. When this turned to death threats, he decided to leave. From there he traveled north and stayed in a Buddhist monastery. The Buddhists accepted him with open arms and called him *Issa*. With their aid, he learned the art of meditation. He spent most of his days in fervent meditation and personal reflection.

After years of intense worship and meditation, he attained a true understanding of God and the world that he lived in. He realized that, throughout the world, Monotheism would ultimately triumph over other forms of worship. He understood it to be a period when true Monotheists would rule the planet, allowing them to live in peace for many years to come. There wouldn't be any forms of suffering such as conflicts or war. Then the spirits of these people would travel to the divine realm. He called this realm *The Kingdom of God*. The many years of peaceful life on earth were referred to as *The Kingdom of God on Earth*. To spread this newfound knowledge, he left the monastery and traveled west. Yeshua finally returned to his homeland at the age of twenty-nine. He preached to the people wherever he camped during this long journey. Once back in Palestine, he first went to John and stayed with his cult for a while. After spending forty days and nights out in the desert, getting lost in deep meditation, he finally decided to go home.

Yeshua went throughout Galilee, teaching in the synagogues and proclaiming the good news of the kingdom. This was a ray of hope for the people, especially those belonging to the lower strata of society. He gave food to the hungry and took care of those in need. Using his knowledge of Ayurveda, he started treating sick people. He also cured the sickness within people through the love and worship of God. He gave the sight of reality to those blinded by the material world. Integrating the wisdom he gained through meditation with the Torah, he taught people the norms and laws that should be observed as a community to improve their morale. Over a very short period, he gained a significant number of followers. He appointed twelve of the most devoted among them to help him preach to a wider audience. They came to be known as the twelve apostles.

Those who followed him saw him as the much-awaited Messiah who was prophesied to come to finally unite the people of Israel. The Jewish messiah concept had its root in the apocalyptic literature of the second century to first century BCE, promising a future leader from the royal lineage, who was expected to be anointed with holy anointing oil and rule the Jewish people during the Messianic Age and world to come. Living with all the oppression and cruelty around them, these people truly believed that the end of the world was soon to come.

Amidst all this, Yeshua's mind always lingered around the displaced tribes of the Kingdom of Israel during and after the Assyrian rule. He felt an intense urge to bring them back to Israel, their true homeland. Later he was able to acquire some of their locations. One day, accompanied by his twelve apostles, Yeshua set out on a voyage westward across the Mediterranean Sea, toward the southern regions of present-day Spain. There he came across one of the lost tribes, the tribe of Gad. He spent a few days with them, teaching them about the one true God and his kingdom. He tried to coerce a few of them to go back to Jerusalem with him. But terrified of the Roman brutality that they might encounter, denied his invitation. Yeshua then returned to Jerusalem.

The teachings of Yeshua came to denounce the practices of the Jewish priests of his time and to reinforce the actual law of God. In the face of a materialistic age of luxury and worship of wealth, Yeshua called his people to a nobler life of worship, love and good deeds. His call, from the beginning, was marked by its complete uprightness and piety. It was based on the principle that there is no mediation between the creator and his creatures. Behind most of his teachings was the message of the coming Kingdom of God, an enigma Yeshua did not attempt to simplify. However, this led him to conflicts with the superficial interpretation of the Torah that existed during his time. He said that he did not come to abrogate the Torah, but to complete it by going to the spirit of its substance to arrive at its essence. Nevertheless, many Jewish priests saw him as a false messiah and treated him with hate and disgust. They had already made an imaginary picture of the Messiah, an earthly king possessing great splendor and authority. But Yeshua did not conform to that imaginary picture, as he was a lowly Jew born in the tiny village of Nazareth.

Chapter Seventeen
The Failed Messiah

The year was 33 CE. Judea was still under Roman occupation. The Jewish religious elite had to answer directly to the new Roman governor, Pontius Pilate. The Roman authorities had appointed Caiphus to the high priesthood, the most prestigious and powerful position a Jew could hold. On the Jewish holiday of Passover, Jerusalem was bursting with religious fervor. It was a holiday that commemorated the creation of the nation and its freedom. With the Roman soldiers standing along the colonnade, Yeshua came to the temple, supported by a large gathering of followers. He drove the cattle herders and dove sellers out, overturned the tables of the money changers, and stood with authority in front of the Romans. This politically charged climate led to a huge revolt. A few days after this incident, Caiphus, under severe pressure from Rome, ordered the arrest of Yeshua and later put him on trial. False accusations arose from every direction. He was hastily convicted by the Jewish elites who despised him, for inciting opposition to the Roman rule. He was then turned in to Pontius Pilate, who ordered that Yeshua be sent to the cross.

Yeshua was handed over to the soldiers for crucifixion. He went calmly with his captors, who tortured him along the way. They reached a place called Golgotha, meaning the Place of Skulls, outside the walls of Jerusalem. Instead of giving him a cup of wine, which was the usual practice, one of the soldiers gave him some sort of herbal formula. Then he was laid on the cross with his arms outstretched. Another soldier came with a five-inch nail and drove it through the palms of his hands, into the crossbeam. After being nailed, he was hoisted up by a rope. Then another longer nail was driven through his feet, placed one

The First Revelation

over the other. He suffered excruciating pain and agony. He fought for breath even when his brain went numb with pain. After some time, he was given another dose of the herbal formula. Following this, he stopped responding. Thinking that he had died, Pilate permitted Yeshua's followers to bring his body down. After wrapping his body in linen, two of his followers took him to a large tomb that had been hewed out of a rock. Just when they laid him down, they realized that he was still alive. Immediately they brought myrrh and aloe for his wounds and tended to him. They took him to one of their houses which was near the tomb. The next day, he regained consciousness and started asking for water.

Crucifixion meant dying on the cross. So, Yeshua was never crucified. He was just hanged on the cross, which he survived.

On the third day after his hanging on the cross, Yeshua was able to walk, but the pain on the nail-driven feet was excruciating. Still, he managed to secretly visit some of his followers to let them know that he was alive. After giving them the proper instructions necessary to spread the message of true Monotheism, Yeshua fled to Damascus, present-day Syria. His mother accompanied him against his will. From there they both traveled east till they crossed the boundaries of the Roman Empire. Yeshua kept going east till he reached some Jewish settlements in present-day Bukhara, Uzbekistan. There he found the lost tribes of Issachar and Naphtali. He moved from one settlement to the next, setting them back on the right path of God.

From there he traveled southeast, across treacherous hilly terrains, to reach a huge Jewish settlement in the region of present-day Peshawar, Pakistan. He realized that it was the center of an extensive population of many lost Israeli tribes spread across the lands of Pakistan, Afghanistan, India and further east. The tribe in power was the tribe of Ephraim. He also met people from the tribe of Reuben, the tribe of Simeon and some from the tribe of Gad. After purifying their faith through his teachings, he traveled further east to a land enclosed by snow-covered mountains on all sides. It was a mountain range with unparalleled alpine beauty. The place was occupied by a group of Jews called the Kasher, from the lost tribe of Asher. He felt that his journey had finally borne fruit. But the onerous journey from Peshawar cost him the life of his beloved mother. She was buried in the region of present-day Murree, Pakistan.

Yeshua decided to live the rest of his life with the tribe of Asher. They called him Yusa. As he often referred to himself as the gatherer of the lost tribes of Israel, he was called *Yusa Asaf*, meaning *Yusa the Gatherer*. He got married and had children. He used to travel to different regions of India. In the region of present-day Mumbai, he came across the tribe of Zebulon and on the Indo-Burma border, he came across the tribe of Manasseh. He successfully found nine among the ten lost tribes of Israel. Only the tribe of Dan was left for him to find. During his travels, he kept on trying to spread his message by staying in Hindu temples and Buddhist monasteries. He was drawn more towards Buddhism, as its basic teachings were monotheistic at the time. His status within the Buddhist community grew to such an extent that he even became the moving force of the Fourth Great Buddhist Council.

One day, at the age of eighty-five, Yeshua realized that his time was about to come. He called one of his disciples and instructed him to build a tomb at the very spot of his death. In his new hometown, along the valley of a tranquil lake, in the shade of an old fig tree, Yeshua delivered his last sermon. The Shepherd left the flock, not being able to achieve his mission of gathering the lost sheep of his ancestors. His spirit was finally raised to the kingdom of his God. However, before his death, Yeshua spoke of another advocate that would come after him, sent by God as a spirit of truth, who would testify to His teachings and guide the misled world to righteousness again.

Chapter Eighteen
Prophet To God

66 CE saw the conversion of a set of rebellions by the Jews against the Romans into a full-fledged war. This went on for years. In the year of 70 CE, under the command of Titus, sixty-thousand Roman soldiers marched towards the city of Jerusalem, eager to slay the Jews. After four months of siege, Titus gave the orders to attack, focusing on the very heart of the city, the sacred second temple. Soldiers poured into the streets, sword in hand. They massacred indiscriminately all whom they met and burned the houses of all who had taken refuge within. Tens of thousands of Jews were not only slaughtered but suffered ignominious violent ends. Alleys were clogged with corpses and the whole city of Jerusalem drowned in blood. Countless others, who survived the war, marched out of the city in chains. The ordeal finally ended with the temple being set ablaze and razed to the ground. The Romans left nothing of the temple which could be a reminder that it once existed. But the Jews who settled outside Jerusalem did their part in the rebellion against Rome during the decades that followed.

In the aftermath of all these revolts, the surviving religious elders slowly altered the very teachings of their faith, to take on more pacifist leanings. This eventually led to the emergence of Rabbinic Judaism by the end of the second century CE. On the other side, followers of Yeshua formed an apocalyptic messianic Jewish sect over the years following his absence. His parables and the stories of his miracles, suffering and death were passed down verbally to the generations that followed. Over time some of these stories were written down and thus gave rise to the first Gospels. These followers travelled far and wide across the Roman Empire, spreading Yeshua's teachings and inviting people into this new Jewish sect. As time passed, the relationship between their sect and others started becoming more and more hostile. Followers of Yeshua accepted the name of Christians, meaning the followers of Christ.

After the advent of Rabbinic Judaism, Christianity became a separate religion altogether. Even within Christians, new sects started to develop as there was an array of Gospels to choose from. Among these, the most prominent ones were Orthodox Christians, Gnostics and Marcionic Christians. By the year 250 CE, early Christianity grew so much that a stronger church organization was needed to administer the welfare system. Meanwhile, Roman rulers felt that their control was slipping away. So, the persecution of Christians reached its peak. But later Christian institutions became so entrenched in Roman society that Christians were found within the army and even the Roman administration. Thus, an edict was passed in the year 311 CE to stop their persecution.

By this time, the entire western Roman Empire was in a state of collapse. There was a total of four emperors who were all trying to make a play for the throne. The Roman Empire was disintegrating. The barbarians were on the borders. One of the four emperors was Constantine. After one last decisive victory, he became the sole ruler of the entire Roman Empire. While trying to unify his Empire, Constantine was plagued by the fact that there were virtually dozens of religious cults to choose from. He knew that to establish an order, only one religion should exist. He worshipped Apollo, the Sun God. But most of the officer corps and Roman elites practiced a religion called Mithraism, which was also a form of sun worship, with Mithras being the son of the Sun God. Among the rest of the population, Orthodox Christianity was the most prominent. Constantine thus plotted one of the greatest and most evil plans in world history.

In 325 CE, Constantine called together the Orthodox bishops of the Roman Empire to form the Council of Nicea. Their goal was to reach a consensus. There, they concluded that Yeshua was equal to God and thus the Nicene Creed took shape. Yeshua's name was also changed to a Greek version, *Iesus*. The bishops needed unity in Christianity and got that unity when the majority agreed that God and Yeshua, whom they called the father and the son, were co-equal. Then Constantine combined Sun worship with early Christianity. The festival of the Sun, which was on 25th December, was declared as Yeshua's date of birth. Most of the rituals in Mithraism were adapted to Christianity. Pagan stories, especially that of the Egyptian god Horus, were used along with the existing life story of Yeshua as proof of his divinity. The bishops had no problem integrating these into the scriptures, as their religion was finally getting recognition. Orthodox Christianity thus changed to Nicene Christianity. Once that happened, all other Christian sects were declared as heretical, and in Rome, it meant death or exile.

This chain of deceit, deception and destruction of the evidence was all to hold the whole thing together around one particular story. To maintain absolute order, any traces of pagan ties to Christianity were also destroyed. The pagan stories were regarded as such a threat because everybody knew that these had some relation to Christianity. Many were put to death or sent into exile, books were burnt, temples were torn down and the symbol of the cross was placed over everything.

In the ancient pagan temple of Serapium in Egypt, members of the Serapis cult were forced to secretly worship statues of their Gods and Goddesses, in dark tunnels deep beneath the earth. On the shelves of its caves were laid religious scrolls and papyri of their cult with similar stories, hidden away for safekeeping. One of those whose job it was to teach the ancient wisdom of these Pagan stories was Hypatia, a Greco-Roman philosopher who lectured at the Serapium. In 401 CE, a Christian mob with the knowledge of Archbishop Cyril persecuted Hypatia in a very cruel manner and burnt her bones to ashes. The Great Library was the greatest collection of human wisdom on the planet at the time. It was completely demolished. All the books that were moved from the Great Library to the Serapium were also burnt and thus history itself was completely erased and rewritten. St Augustine declared that now that they had the scriptures, they didn't need anything else. Thus, all the other Gospels were destroyed and only the four accepted by Orthodox Christianity survived.

Christianity thus became a part of the imperial establishment. Constantine showed his support through massive construction projects, especially in Jerusalem. Constantine claimed that he was a Christian while he still publicly worshipped Apollo, the Sun God. In the year 382 CE, next to the church of Nativity, in a secret underground cave, the first official translation of the Latin New Testament Bible was prepared. With the help of two nuns, it was written by Church Father and Bible scholar St Jerome. By 476 CE, the western Roman Empire had fallen. But orthodox Christianity flourished throughout the west and kept on spreading. Constantine's insistence on a literal Jesus was the law. The cross which was a dejected symbol of death and defeat became a symbol of triumph. In the eyes of some, the apocalyptic prophecy of revelation had at last been fulfilled. Yeshua of Nazareth, who was an anti-Roman rebel of the Gospels, thus became Jesus Christ, a symbol of Roman imperialism. Christianity became the dominant religion of the world and the Church became the greatest power on earth.

The world today sees Jesus as the Son of God and a vast majority of Christians see him as the one true God itself. Thus, Christianity turned itself into a paganistic and polytheistic religion, worshipping human beings embodying God and various saints. There is no doubt that Jesus was one of the most successful and influential people in the history of mankind, who provided an invisible yet adamantine link between the new world religions of Judaism, Christianity, Islam and even Buddhism. Perhaps this is why he made a promise to his followers that he would come again. Through one of his unidentified descendants, his spirit could make another appearance in this material realm, to finally complete his mission of bringing together his people. He might become a great spiritual leader and unite the people, by spreading the absolute truth of God, abolishing all these religious groups that fight with each other, and establishing a universal religion based on true Monotheism. As a result, he could finally create the Kingdom of God on Earth. So, let us also wait alongside millions of Christians, for the second coming of Jesus, the promised human Messiah.

Chapter Nineteen
Ruling The Desert

Through Yishmael, Abram's first son, the harsh deserts of the land of Arabia gave birth to the Arabian civilization. Abram and Ishmael together built a great cubical shrine at the heart of the land, as a center of true Monotheism. The cubical shrine made of stone was called *Ka'ba*. The Monotheists who followed Abram and Ishmael called themselves the Hanifs. Their one true God was Aażah, the god of Abram, whose name later became *Allah* when the Arabic language developed. Kaaba was blessed with a perennial spring just near it and through this, the region surrounding the shrine became a large city over the centuries. However, the growth of the civilization was sluggish as they were in the middle of a desert without any valuable natural resources. But Kaaba remained a great pilgrimage center for all the people residing in the deserts of Arabia and the city of Mecca grew with it. As more time passed, like in all other cultures, there was a shift from Monotheism to polytheism and paganism.

The society was mostly nomadic, inhabited by constantly moving tribal units. There were constantly shifting alliances, leading to never-ending warfare. These tribes placed heavy emphasis on family, and would roam through the deserts with their kin in groups, along with their livestock, living in tents. Their culture was patriarchal, with the inheritance passing on to the male offspring, while the women were treated as commodities. Unlimited polygamy and female infanticide were far too common. There were no written laws, courts or law enforcement of any kind to protect the people. Vengeance was sought for the killing of a tribal member by another tribe, which led to constant conflicts and warfare. The only rules that existed within a tribe were those enforced by the tribal leaders. In short, lawlessness was the law of the land of Arabia.

By the end of the fifth century CE, new gods or goddesses sprang out of nowhere and were viewed as guardians of individual tribes. As well as being the site of an annual pilgrimage, the Kaaba in Mecca housed a total of three hundred sixty idols of tribal patron deities. Jewish and Christian populations also started to emerge in the Arab region. The Hanifs in Arabia thus reduced to a very small number. The whole of Arabia was dominated by the Quraysh tribe, one of the few settled tribes in Arabia. Being direct descendants of Abram through Yishmael, they controlled the sacred Kaaba and the city of Mecca. They formed a cult of the Arabian nomads, which tied members of many tribes in Arabia to the Kaaba. To counter the effects of anarchy, Quraysh upheld the institution of sacred months of pilgrimage during which all violence was forbidden, so that it was possible to participate in pilgrimages without fear. So, despite the fact that this action's primary motivation was religious, it also had significant economic ramifications for the city of Mecca and, consequently, for the tribe of Quraysh, whose succeeding leaders developed greater avarice. From this powerful tribe of Quraysh, in the year 570 CE, a great spiritual and political leader was born. His beloved grandfather named him Muhammed.

Muhammed's father had passed away before his birth and his mother was impoverished. When Muhammed was just a few months old, due to inadequate production of breast milk, she was forced to hand him over to a wet nurse living on the outskirts of Mecca. As a result, he lived a nomadic life for the first four years of his life. At the age of five, he returned to his mother. But a year later, he lost his mother during a return journey from her family in Yathrib. The orphaned Muhammad was taken in by his grandfather who took the most tender care of him. However, the old chief of Quraysh died two years later. On his deathbed, he confided the charge of the little orphan to his son and Muhammed's uncle, Abu Talib. Abu Talib was also a powerful figure among the leaders of Quraysh. He was a trader taking caravans to

The First Revelation

Syria, part of a business which connected the desert life of Arabia to the populous centers and civilizations beyond its borders. This greatly influenced Muhammed who also used to accompany his uncle on many of his travels. Muhammed heard stories about other people with alien cultures and different faiths. He was greatly influenced by the Hanifs, who followed the strict Monotheism taught by his greatest ancestors. Unlike his fellow pagan tribe members, he decided to become a Monotheist and accepted Allah as the one true God. But his heart was still stung by the grief of losing all those dear to him at such a young age.

Muhammed was highly respected for his correctness of manners and purity of morals which were rare among the people of Mecca. His fair character helped him acquire the nickname *Al-Ameen*, meaning *The Faithful*. He also became the leader of a trade caravan. His reputation attracted a proposal in 595 CE from Khadijah, a successful widowed businesswoman, who was fifteen years older than him. Muhammad consented to the marriage, which, by all accounts, was a happy one. Through Khadija, he had children, and they led a peaceful family life. But the male children died in childhood. His disgust for the concept of death returned. He was also not content with the ways of the world. The horrible treatment of the downtrodden people in society deeply disturbed him. Muhammed started to make regular spiritual retreats to one of the highest mountains in Mecca, to seek peace, and to pray to his one true God.

Muhammed's spiritual retreats became more fervid and ever more frequent. He could spend hours, even whole days and nights, devoted to intense meditation and prayer. In 610 CE, during one of his meditation sessions, an unexpected dreadful spiritual experience overtook him. It was similar to someone tearing the soul out of his body. This made him tremble in fear. He ran home and sought his beloved wife Khadija. After getting to know about the incident, Khadija took the issue to her cousin Waraqah, who was a Christian and a renowned Biblical scholar. He assured her that there was nothing

The First Revelation

wrong with Muhammed and that it could have been a spiritual experience similar to those of the prophets in Christianity and Judaism. However, this horrible experience led to his first spiritual revelation.

The initial revelation was followed by a three-year pause, during which Muhammad felt depressed and further gave himself to prayers and spiritual practices. When the revelations resumed, he was reassured and decided to begin preaching these to others, first to his family members and then to his trusted companions. These revelations were all based on true Monotheism. He memorized these revelations and recited them verbatim to his followers. After a few months, he began to preach to the public. As Muhammed's teachings were completely against idolatry and polytheism, the leaders of Quraysh felt threatened. Their wealth was entirely dependent on the wide variety of idols that were worshipped within and around the Kaaba. First, they tried to persuade him by offering him wealth and power. When this didn't work out, gentle persuasion got replaced by violent persecution. Muhammed and his followers were attacked in public, both verbally and physically. Muhammed had clan protection under Abu Talib. But those with no clan or tribal protection were subjected to brute force. Some were even beaten and stabbed to death. Therefore, such people left Mecca and sought refuge in an Ethiopian kingdom across the Red Sea.

Back in Mecca, the Quraysh were incensed by this exodus. They executed different plans to bring them back, all of which failed. Muhammed went on with his mission of preaching to the people even under severe persecution. But the year of 619 CE gave rise to one of the most devastating times of his life. Muhammed's pillar of strength and his crown jewel, his wife Khadija, passed away. Muhammed was devastated. A few months after this, he was hit by another devastating loss. This time it was his uncle Abu Talib. With Abu Talib gone, Muhammed lost his clan's support. The Quraysh leaders finally had the perfect opportunity to kill him. Knowing the danger, half of his

The First Revelation

followers fled to Ethiopia, and the rest were almost in hiding in Mecca.

It was during this time that Muhammed underwent the most intense spiritual experience of his life where he got to perceive God in very close proximity. His soul entered a new realm of divine revelation. This helped him to abandon the tribal sentiments which had their roots deep within him. With his life already in danger, he decided to finally leave Mecca with his followers. People from Yathrib had already asked him to join their community as he had previously acted as an arbitrator in some of their communal conflicts. He and his followers thus left Mecca for Yathrib, hoping for a fresh start. After the arrival of Muhammed, Yathrib was renamed *Medina*.

The community in Medina was made up of several different tribes. Some were Pagan Arabs, some were Jewish, and there were also Christians. Because of this great diversity, the city was plagued by warfare and constant feuding between the local tribes. This had a significant impact on the growth of the community. By being a part of this community, it became easier for Muhammed to solve their conflicts. With the help of his followers, he built the first temple for prayer in Medina. The first call to prayer was made by a freed African slave who had endured the most brutal persecution in Mecca.

The new temple also acted as a community center. Everyone residing in Medina came to the temple to solve their issues, including Jews and Christians. Muhammed thus laid the foundations for a reformed community in Medina based on ideology rather than kinship. As his role within this community grew, he prepared an agreement with a set of written laws that formalized his role in Medina. It became one of the earliest written constitutions in the world. It laid out the duties and rights of the citizens, as well as the responsibilities of those that govern them. This further strengthened Muhammed's relationship with the various tribes in Medina.

Although Muhammed and his followers were free from the torture

The First Revelation

they faced in Mecca, their enemies still sought to destroy them. In the year 624 CE, Muhammed came to know that a large Quraysh army was coming towards Medina. He finally decided to retaliate against the never-ending oppression his people faced. A small army was forged and certain rules were laid down for a just war. Under these rules, unarmed civilians including women and children were not to be hurt, the prisoners of war were not to be killed, and if their opponents were to ask for peace, the war was to be stopped. The rules also laid stress on non-aggression, proper declaration, right intention, war as a last resort, proportional retaliation and strict adherence to covenants. With these rules in their head and with the faith of God in their hearts, the army of Muhammed went out to face an army three times their size. The Quraysh army was defeated. For Muhammed and his followers, the victory was a great vindication of the faith that had sustained them over the past fourteen years.

Almost a year after the first battle, the Quraysh leaders returned to Medina with a new and bigger army than before. This war almost resulted in a stalemate. But Muhammed lost some of his closest companions and greatest fighters to this war. A third and final battle took place in 627 CE when an army of ten thousand Quraysh soldiers charged towards the city of Medina. Muhammed came to know about the ambush beforehand and dug a huge trench across the only passageway into the city of Medina, which was surrounded by large volcanic hills on all the other sides. The Quraysh cavalry found it impossible to get past the trench. After multiple attempts, the army eventually withdrew to Mecca. Following this war, Muhammed became the official ruler of Medina. He made radical changes to the tribal customs of Medina. He abolished the brutal tradition of blood feuds. Women acquired a share of the inheritance and secured rights to own property. In short, a moral code was constructed based on the idea of social justice for all. But the Quraysh leaders still posed a huge threat to Medina. Muhammed also needed to spread his teachings outside its boundaries. That is when he received the greatest revelation that would change the course of world history.

Chapter Twenty
Revenge Is Sweet

Although Muhammed succeeded in thwarting all the Quraysh invasions, they were still powerful and in control of Mecca. He always knew that he was not strong enough to overcome them militarily. Therefore, he had to undermine them politically. He formed alliances with other tribes across Arabia through trade and even marriage. His influence started growing more and more. Then he made one final move. He set out to his homeland accompanied by his followers as pilgrims. Unarmed and on foot, they journeyed through the stark and harsh environment of the desert, fighting the searing heat. But they were stopped about eight miles outside of the city by a group of Quraysh cavalry. As it was against the law to attack an unarmed pilgrim, they had no other option but to negotiate with Muhammed. A formal agreement was finally made. Quraysh leaders insisted that Muhammed and his followers return to Medina without performing the pilgrimage. In return, they would stop the attacks and would allow Muhammed and his followers to perform the pilgrimage in the following year. Muhammed signed the agreement. His followers saw the treaty as a humiliating defeat. But he assured them that it was a manifest victory.

In February 629 CE, Muhammed and his followers set out for a second time to perform the pilgrimage. When they saw the Kaaba right in front of them after a long wait of seven years, their eyes filled with tears of joy. Then they performed the pilgrimage with utmost faith and devotion. This fostered a change in the perception of Meccans towards them. The Meccans witnessed the people whom they saw as barbarians sincerely taking part in the pilgrimage. The status of Muhammed among the Meccans thus evolved. This enraged the

The First Revelation

Quraysh leaders. They broke the treaty the following year by attacking some of Muhammad's followers who were out preaching in the desert. Muhammed realized that the only way out of this was by fighting back. He gathered a massive army of about ten thousand men and marched towards Mecca.

The Quraysh, who had now lost most of their alliances to Muhammed, realized that they couldn't resist the attack. They expected Muhammed and his men to storm into the city and organize a bloody massacre after many years of oppression and persecution. Seeing the massive army, the Meccans started fleeing their homes. However, the army of Muhammed seized control over the city without shedding a single drop of blood. Instead, the men paved the way for Muhammed to enter the Kaaba. All the idols of gods and goddesses placed inside the Kaaba were taken out and turned to rubble. Muhammed thus took over the city of Mecca with peace. He granted amnesty to the Quraysh leaders and thus drowned the criticism of his enemies with kindness. He then left the city of his birth and returned to Medina, his adopted home.

Muhammed's bloodless conquest of Mecca was clear proof that his movement was succeeding. This attracted a large number of followers. By 631 CE, the last of the pagan tribes fell, having converted to true Monotheism, and Muhammed thus became the ruler of the whole of Arabia. He created an Arabia which provided both peace and security to its people. In 632 CE, he performed his last pilgrimage to Mecca. He then gave what became known as his farewell sermon. In this, Muhammed spoke of the right to life and property, the rights of women, and the necessity of prayer, fasting and charity. He also said that no human being has superiority over another human, whether it be based on race, caste or culture. Following this, he returned home to Medina. On 8th June 632 CE, Muhammed breathed his last in the house of his wife Aisha, surrounded by thousands of his followers who kept praying to the one true God with eyes filled with tears.

Muhammed thus laid the foundations of Islam, which later spread across the globe. Adherents of Islam came to be known as Muslims. For about two billion Muslims worldwide, Muhammed is the last and greatest of the long line of prophets who have brought the word of God to humanity. The Quran, which Muslims believe to be the direct word of God, was his greatest contribution to the world. It remains preserved in its pure unaltered form, unlike other religious scriptures. It lays down laws and commandments, codes for social and moral behavior, and contains a comprehensive religious philosophy. Yet, some people used the text as the basis for violent ideology. They took certain verses which were in the context of the wars that took place in Islamic history, and used it to justify an extremist political philosophy, leading to terrorism. But for the vast majority of Muslims who live by the Quran, its messages of peace and compassion are its true guiding principle.

Throughout history, Muslims have striven to live based on the teachings of the Quran. But over time, they began placing more emphasis on Hadiths, which were based on easily falsifiable accounts of the life of Muhammad. Muslim scholars used a mixture of Quranic verses and passages from Hadiths to create their version of Sharia or Islamic law. The Arabic word Islam means submission to one God. Therefore, it was always meant to be a religion which emphasizes true Monotheism. The Quran does not give any statement that authentic Muslims are only those who acknowledge Muhammad as a prophet. Based on its definition, all those who believe in the one true God are Muslims or adherents of Islam. Sadly, like every other religion, Islam also slowly became a separate faith, claiming that only its people are God's chosen ones.

Chapter Twenty-One
One Final Battle

After the death of Muhammad, his closest companion Abu Bakr was elected as the leader of Arabia. The vast deserts of Arabia were sandwiched between the Roman-Byzantine Empire to the west and Persian-Sasanian Empire to the east. Just when these two empires thought that they were indestructible, the Arab army swept in on them like a human tsunami. In speed and extent, the first Arab conquests were unmatched. They kept on laying siege to every city that that they encountered. This happened simultaneously in every direction. The once-dominant Byzantine and Sassanid empires continued to lose wars and cities like dominoes, toppling one after another. Arabia quickly grew into an empire, which called itself the Rashidun Caliphate. The emperor was called the Caliph.

The First Revelation

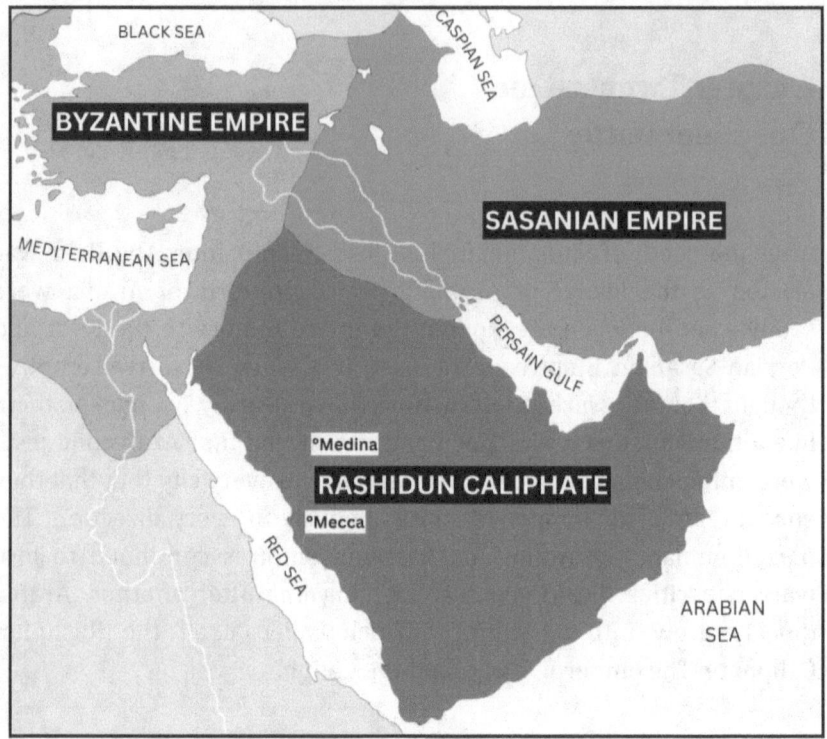

Arabia under Rashidun caliphate in 632 CE

One of the most notable victories was the conquest of Jerusalem in 638 CE, which the Muslims also regarded as a sacred place. Instead of a direct ambush, the Arab army laid siege to the city, preventing commerce and communication. After a long wait of two years, the Roman army garrisoned inside the city had no option but to surrender. Following the conquest of the Achaemenid Empire, it was the first time the city got conquered without any bloodshed. The then Caliph, Umar, proposed for all Christian businesses, assets and Churches to be retained and promised that the Arab army would not plunder the city. Umar also requested for the Jewish population of Jerusalem to be reinstated, having previously been purged by the Roman army. He was able to find eighty Jewish families and resettled them in the city.

The First Revelation

The Arab conquest went on for centuries under the banner of different caliphates. The fall of the Sasanian Empire was abrupt. By 651 CE, the empire was dissolved and most of its territories were absorbed by the Arabian Caliphate. Later, new empires started to emerge under the banner of Islam. The Byzantine Empire held on for a long period against these caliphates and empires until its capital was conquered by the Ottoman Empire in 1453 CE. This marked the end of the Byzantine Empire. When the spread of Islam reached its peak, there were three mighty empires to its name. The Ottoman Empire occupied most of the Middle East and many of the western territories which belonged to the Byzantines. The Safavid Empire occupied Persia and Central Asia. The Mughals carved out an empire stretching from the borders of Persia in the west to the Bay of Bengal in the east. All these three empires became known as the Gunpowder Empires as the use of guns for warfare was marked as a vital factor for their power.

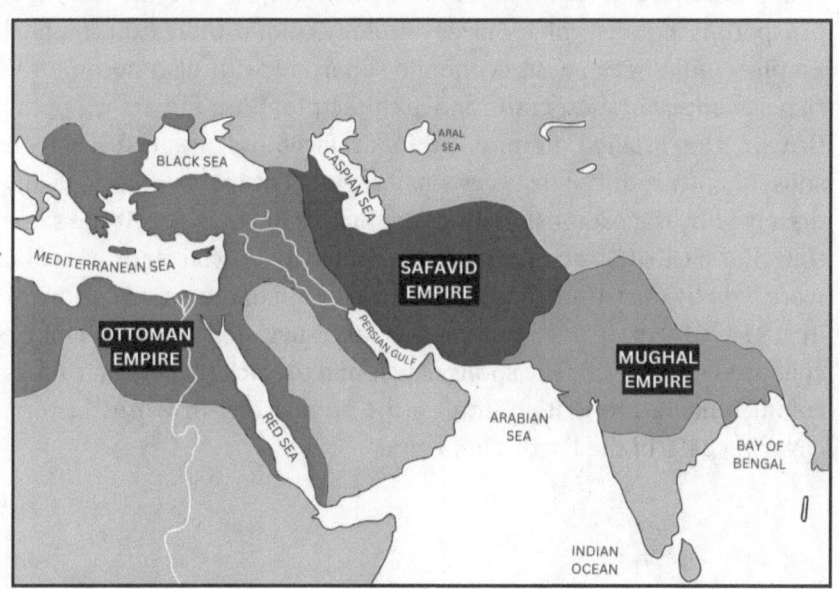

The Gunpowder Empires at the height of their dominance

The later Islamic emperors became extremely corrupt due to their insatiable hunger for wealth and power. They started forced conversion and destruction of the temples of other religious faiths, which was seen as a terrible sin in Islam. This caused their empires to crumble from within. At the same time, this turned out to be a great boon for the powers that were emerging in the west. These new western empires discovered a new way of conquering foreign lands from within. They would initially gain entry into these lands in the name of trade. Then they would slowly dispossess the indigenous inhabitants and institute legal control over them. In the end, the land, its people and its vast resources would be under their grasp. This started the age of colonization.

Many empires in the west competed with each other to colonize foreign lands outside of their territories. These mainly included the British Empire, the Dutch Empire, the Portuguese Empire and the Spanish Empire. Among them, the British Empire became the most prosperous because of its largest colony, India. Under the Mughal Empire, India became an economic superpower. It also became the richest center for arts, crafts and architecture. With the arrival of the British, the Mughal Empire in India faced its greatest rival. It subsequently reduced to a very small region. The empire was formally dissolved by the establishment of the British Raj in India. At the same time, Russia, Britain and Germany competed for crucial territories that were held by the Ottomans. This eventually led to the First World War in 1914 CE. In its aftermath, the last surviving Muslim empire collapsed in 1918 CE. The spoils of war and the rich resources from its colonies made the British Empire the largest one in world history, covering 24% of the Earth's land area.

The First Revelation

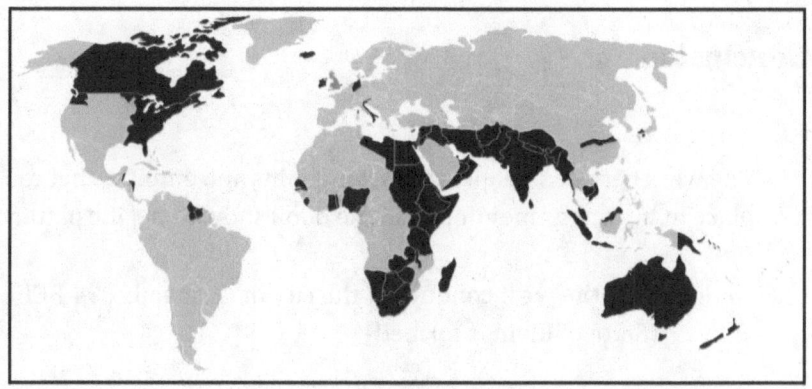

British empire at its greatest extent in 1920 CE

Failure to manage the instability that resulted from the upheaval after the First World War contributed to the outbreak of the Second World War in 1939 CE. Although Britain and its empire emerged victorious from this, the effects of the conflict were profound, both at home and abroad. Much of Europe, a continent that had dominated the world for several centuries, was left in ruins. The balance of global power shifted to the United States and the Soviet Union. At the same time, anti-colonial movements were on the rise in the colonies of all European empires. Britain dealt with the most severe blow. By 1981 CE, aside from a scattering of islands and outposts, the process of decolonization that had begun after the Second World War was largely complete. The handover of Britain's last major and most populous overseas territory, Hong Kong, to China in 1997 CE marked the end of the British Empire.

Conclusion

The wars between people, cities, kingdoms and empires that took place in history as mentioned in the book show a specific pattern.

- Awanites from the west conquered the city of Anshan [2894 BCE]
    (State of Elam is formed)

- Anshanites from the east conquered the state of Elam [2700 BCE]
    (Kingdom of Sumer and State of Akkad is formed)

- Akkadians from the west conquered the Kingdom of Sumer [2334 BCE]
    (Akkadian Empire is formed)

- Sumerians and Elamites from the east conquered the Akkadian Empire [2112 BCE]
    (Neo-Sumerian Empire is formed)

- Hurrians and Amorites from the west conquered the Neo-Sumerian Empire [1894 BCE]
    (Babylonian Empire is formed)

- Arameans and Kassites from the east conquered the Babylonian Empire [1531 BCE]
    (Neo-Assyrian Empire gets formed over centuries)

- Phrygians from the west conquered the Neo-Assyrian Empire [612 BCE]
    (Neo-Babylonian Empire is formed)

- Persians from the east conquered the Neo-Babylonian Empire [539 BCE]
    (Achaemenid Empire is formed)

- Greeks from the west conquered Achaemenid Empire [330 BCE]
    (Roman Empire is formed over centuries)

- Muslims from the east conquered Roman Empire [633 - 1453 CE]
    (Many Islamic empires emerge throughout the world)

- Europeans from the west colonized the Islamic empires [1500 - 1918 CE]
    (British Empire expands to become the largest empire in history)

It can be clearly understood that all the conflicts occurred between an evil non-monotheistic power in the west and a comparatively good monotheistic power in the east. First, the non-monotheistic power in the west attacked the east and dominated them. However, the defeated monotheistic power in the east flourished and slowly took over the west. Then the non-monotheistic power further spread west and struck back with revenge. This pattern has repeated throughout history. In this vicious cycle, cities were formed by groups of people. These cities came together to form states, which, in turn, gave rise to kingdoms. These kingdoms then came under one single power and became an empire. In the end, all these empires came together under the banner of religion. Throughout all of this, Monotheism kept on spreading and pushing all other forms of belief further west. Is this pattern in history a mere coincidence? Or is it a sign of something bigger, maybe a divine intervention?

The pattern last ended with the defeat of the east by western colonizers dismantling its culture, looting all of its resources and exploiting its valuable manpower. But the throne of the western empires was short-lived. It broke down and now a new power is spreading slowly throughout the west incognito. It is the ideology of true Monotheism. The clear-sighted modern generation is breaking the sturdy barriers built by religions and is accepting the fact that there is only one God, and that this God is the same for all religions. For them, the name is becoming irrelevant.

Some historians claim that Monotheism is a recent trend in the evolution of human history and it has its origin in Judaism or Zoroastrianism. But there is clear archaeological evidence to support the fact that Monotheism has always existed in history for a very long time, even before the formation of these religions. It just started from a single point in ancient history and kept spreading through certain enlightened individuals who understood the message of true Monotheism through their acts of intense worship which raised the level of their basic human consciousness. These enlightened individuals emerged in the form of teachers, priests, redeemers, prophets, buddhas or messengers. As they didn't allow their followers to make statues and portraits of themselves, their real faces still remain shrouded to the outside world.

The mission of all these enlightened individuals was the same: to ignite the spark of Monotheism that is present deep within each and every human being. They preached the same message in different ways and introduced distinct ways of worshipping the same creator entity. However, their message was widely misconstrued through time. Subsequent ignorant followers formed separate sects, which appeared to make them special and unique to the rest of the world. These factions fought hard and invented miracle stories to bolster their argument that the so-called founder of their sect is greater than the others. Many even raised these individuals to the position of God. They later became more detached from the true message and formed the new world religions that fight with each other, carrying the badge of 'The Only Truth' with utmost pride.

The blood throbbing in the veins of every human being is the same, thick red. We are all made up of the same matter or energy. And yet, we divide ourselves into separate groups just because our ways of reaching out to that same creator force or entity called God is different. These groups were initially built on the foundation of morality and preached the doctrine of peace. Later, they started using selected misinterpreted verses from their religious scriptures as justification for conquering lands through bloodshed. This eventually led to an era of religious extremism rife with terror and violent slaughter. Due to this, the modern world got lost in a bewildering ideological battle between religious fundamentalists.

So, what is this true Monotheism?

It is the absolute belief in one God and one God only, without the association of any partners. It doesn't matter if you call this one God by any name like Allah, Elaha, Ahura Mazda, Yahweh, Devi or Brahman. You can even prefer not to call God by a name and see this entity as a form of imperceptible higher dimensional conscious energy from which the entire universe including us took form. Therefore, all that matters is the fundamental understanding that God is a single omnipotent conscious entity which is the ultimate creator and overseer of everything that we can perceive around us.

What is the purpose of this?

The main purpose of true Monotheism is understanding this one true God. God is something that is much beyond the theories or concepts that our five limited senses can comprehend. The only way we can understand God is through our human consciousness, which distinguishes us from other living and non-living things. It also leads to the development of free will, which enables us to differentiate between the good and the bad. In religion and spirituality, it is called the human soul or spirit. We need to raise the energy level of this human consciousness beyond a certain level. Only then we can truly begin to understand God. This is exactly the concept of Moksha talked about in the Vedic scriptures, and Nirvana taught by Buddha. One can only raise the energy level of his/her human consciousness through worship, love and good deeds. If you devotedly study all the major monotheistic world religions, it can be derived with certainty that these three things form the core of their basic teachings.

How to properly understand God?

The first is through worship. In today's fast-paced modern society, where people race about like savages seeking money, the typical person has over six thousand thoughts every day. Some researchers suggest that it can even go beyond sixty thousand. The bulk of these are negative and repetitive thoughts that have absolutely no bearing on human existence whatsoever. Even if a person attempts to restrain these thoughts, it becomes nearly impossible since additional thoughts begin to flood their mind. As a result, the human brain never receives adequate rest while awake. This is where meditation and other forms of worship come into play. These practices assist us in quieting our minds, thereby relaxing our brains. Once we have mastered our minds, we need to start trying to connect with God. It might take us days or months or years to properly take control of our mind and further establish that connection. It all depends on the intensity of our worship and the amount of time we invest in it. Mastering our minds, in turn, allows us to acquire more knowledge about the world that we live in.

The second way to understand God is through love. This is not the romantic love that is embellished in plays or movies. This is the love that a person should develop for the whole universe with its every piece of elementary particles. It is the understanding that everyone and everything has value and place in our integral reality. It also acts as a rudder that steers people towards kindness, compassion and appreciation. This feeling of love should be more evident when it comes to fellow human beings, no matter how good or bad they seem to us. Love is the force that binds one human soul to another. When we spread this love to all those around us, we come one step closer to understanding God, thereby experiencing true happiness. The third and final way is through good deeds or good actions. It defines how we live our lives in this material world. Sadly, we all have become deeply addicted to the material things and concepts around us like money, power and status. We use money to gain power over others, and to convince ourselves and society that we are at a higher status compared to others. We don't realize that these things become irrelevant the moment this material body that we reside in stops functioning and becomes one with the earth. Good deeds and actions thus complete the triad of the ways one can understand God. You need to live a pious life by performing only good deeds like helping others, giving charity or even something as simple as smiling at someone. This also involves all those actions that are aimed at being a physically healthy individual. Good deeds thus further strengthen the field of love that we build around us and in turn, help us to connect to God in a better way.

In short, using our mind, we can attain true knowledge through worship; using our heart, we can attain true happiness through love; and using our body, we can attain ideal health through good deeds. These three things need to come together. Once mind, heart and body align themselves together towards God through worship, love and good deeds, a person gets to experience true enlightenment or nirvana.

For some rational minds, these ideas can appear to be nonsensical, especially those who have blind faith in the religion of science. Even the latest scientific theories, which include quantum field theory and string theory, have their arrows pointed towards the possible existence of a conscious creator entity. Now the probable question will be 'How can you prove it?' Also, for those readers who understood the pattern of war between the east and the west, the question will be 'What happens when the whole west comes under true Monotheism?'

The First Revelation

These questions will be answered. Readers can either embark on their own personal journey to unravel the mystery or patiently wait for further revelations.

In the meantime, let us all burn the religious labels that we proudly adorn on our chests, and unite under the banner of humanity, believing in a single all-powerful creator entity. Let us bring down the walls of hatred and connect with each other, practicing compassion and altruism. Instead of putting in effort to prove that one's personal belief system is the only true reality, let us invest that time and effort in addressing the actual problems faced by the world today, including climate change, economic inequality, gender inequality, lack of education, global health issues, food insecurity, water contamination, and human rights violation. Only through this can we finally achieve the dream of a Kingdom of God on Earth.

You can contact the publisher at:
www.fanatixxpubication.com

www.ingramcontent.com/pod-product-compliance
Lightning Source LLC
LaVergne TN
LVHW030324070526
838199LV00069B/6549